THE BIG CHARMER

BOSSY HEARTS
BOOK 2

EVEY LYON

This boss's charm is all it takes for the nanny to be in trouble…

Logan Jax probably shouldn't have eyed the nanny like she was his next meal. But what guy living a bachelor's life wouldn't when Sadie looks like that? He doesn't get points for asking Sadie to be his fake date, either. But he needed to close a billion-dollar deal. And he certainly doesn't get bonus points for sleeping with the nanny. However, Sadie's hand roamed, his hand roamed, and the stars aligned for orgasmic bliss.

His sister gave him one rule when his nephew was placed in his care. Don't (literally) screw up the arrangement with the supernanny.

Despite Sadie trying to keep it professional, his charm wears her down and although Sadie struts around in his shirt, clearly enjoying his cocky antics—it's a problem. She wants him, and he wants her. But Logan Jax doesn't do relationships or family; he isn't the settling-down type, and that's exactly what she wants…

LOGAN

"Wow, so you just ditched her like that? Ballsy move," my friend Cole reminds me.

"I'm not that big of an ass, I got her a fruit basket," I explain to him, as to the reason why I ditched Natalie a month or so back. It was purely sex, nothing more. She was okay with that, and our time as friends with benefits together ran its course. Fruit baskets are my go-to as a goodbye—I mean, at least it's not the cliché flowers, right?

"Logan Jax, you are too much of a gentleman. More than I would have been." Cole looks at me with a knowing grin as he downs his smooth scotch before leaning back on the sofa.

We're both in our suits and enjoying Friday-afternoon drinks at the Grand, a private club and hotel that our parents belong to. For some godforsaken reason, we felt it would be great to continue on the legacy by gaining our own memberships, as young professionals who'd already made seven figures by the time we hit age thirty.

But the place has high ceilings, mahogany wood, classic cocktail hour, and the chef is phenomenal. An aura of classic twenties Chicago, and the views over Lake Michigan are second to none.

It's not like we're complete yuppies; the club has an amazing pool, and the gym alone makes it all worth it. Not to mention, for entertaining business, this place is a must.

I smooth my dark red tie against my crisp white shirt. It was a long week in the office, causing me to sigh as I recall in my head the back-to-back negotiations. I've been trying to close a deal with a new client for the hedge fund that I manage.

"I'm heading to a Cubs game this weekend, want to join?" Cole asks as he indicates to the bar for another drink. He's been my friend since college, which means we've been friends for years.

"Would love to, man, but I can't. My life is about to get fucking complicated." My hand glides through my partially gelled hair before sliding along my jaw with its five-o'clock shadow.

"Shit, is that still happening?" Cole asks, with his intense eyes and a sympathetic look.

I swirl the neat scotch in my glass. "Yep." The P pops from my lips.

My sister Zoe is amazing. As far as sisters go, she is pretty kickass—keeps me in line and calls me on my shit. She is also about to drop out a pair of twins. They will be welcomed with open arms into the family, but let's not have any illusions. They were a surprise. A seven-years-later surprise. I can say that because my nephew Mason is seven years old, and for years I heard my sister relish the fact that she only had one child and that was all she wanted. Then seven months ago, *bam!* She got life-changing news—times two.

With my brain working overtime, I recall how I've come

into this scenario. My nephew's douchebag of a father is no longer in the picture, and the twins' father is new to the scene but is stationed overseas in the military. Zoe is on bedrest in the hospital until the babies come out, and my nephew is a little smarty-pants that got into one of the best summer camps in the city. It's a big deal, as he had some issues in school. This all means good old Uncle Logan was volunteered to harbor Mason for the summer.

"This is going to be a buzzkill on my dating life," I comment as I line up all the logistics in my head. Calling it a dating life is a stretch, since I don't let emotions get involved. I'm not the anchor-down type of guy. I don't picture myself with a wife and kids, and for many women, that's a big problem.

"Absolutely. I mean, how will you even have time for your nephew? With your work schedule and all."

I shrug a shoulder. "My sister arranged a nanny or babysitter or tutor—I don't know what you call someone who picks up the kid from camp and helps him with reading. That means I only really need to worry about mornings. I mean, I don't know. It's the least I can do. My sister needs the help, and Mason is a pretty cool kid."

Cole smirks and winks at me. "Maybe it'll be a hot nanny."

"I hope so, otherwise it may be a long summer." I grin to myself.

We each order a steak for an early dinner, discuss stocks, and as soon as we sign the bill, we head out. As we're descending the stairs in the main hall, we're stopped.

"Jax and Tate," a voice calls out to us.

We both turn to the older man in a suit.

"Mr. Malone." Cole offers his hand, and I follow the protocol.

We know a lot of people here, either through our parents or simply because everyone is aware that we're killing it career-wise.

"Are you both just leaving?" the man asks.

"We are, just came for a post-work drink and bite," Cole explains.

My eyes wander to the women behind Mr. Malone.

"That's a shame," Mr. Malone says. "We could have had a drink outside and enjoyed the summer evening, maybe crack out a cigar. My daughter is here with a friend, and I'm sure they'll get bored with just me," he mentions.

Cole glances at me and we share a look, knowing we're getting our balls busted, because you don't turn down drinks with Winston Malone, not when Cole is eyeing to take over his logistics company for his portfolio.

And definitely not when I further examine the beauties that are standing behind Mr. Malone, completely uninterested in his words but most definitely checking us out. Ruby, I've met a few times. Definitely easy on the eyes with her black hair and green eyes.

But quite frankly, my X-ray vision is focused on the woman next to her, already eyeing the legs attached to the killer body and head of reddish-brown hair. She seems to be classically beautiful, with a simple blue dress that the older members of the club would call respectable—but I call it hot as fuck.

Those eyes must be hazel or some mystical color that I have never witnessed. Her glance meets mine, and this woman is confident. She doesn't blush, and that's what normally happens when a woman finds herself on the receiving end of my gaze.

"What the heck, we aren't in a rush, right?" I mention to Cole, and he nods in agreement.

Winston Malone puts his hands together. "Wonderful. You've met Ruby, my daughter, and this is her friend Sadie Bay."

We all shake hands, yet when I shake Sadie's, I swear the earth stops spinning on its axis. Her hands are soft and delicate, but something tells me they have a hidden talent. Her wry smile is subtle yet enough for me to imagine the many shapes her lips could form.

Letting her hand go, I follow everyone back up the stairs.

Sadie Bay is a name that has a perfect melody, and she has a sway to match.

Fucking fantastic.

And when my mind registers how to work these situations, I thank my chivalrous moves for sending Natalie packing on the friends-with-benefits exit strategy all those weeks ago, because I know over the next few minutes, Cole is going to need to discuss business with Winston, which means I need to entertain the ladies.

Not a problem. I've got this.

Within five minutes, we have a fresh round of drinks—whiskey for the men and gin and tonics for the ladies. Cole and Winston dive straight into conversation, standing at the corner of the deck that is on the sixteenth floor. I sit with the ladies at a table nearby.

Here I go. Charm the ladies.

"A special occasion today or just wanted to have dinner with your old man?" I ask.

Ruby smiles as she puts her phone down. "I'm in town, and Sadie and I went to high school together. She just moved to the city, so we just spent the day exploring the city and shopping."

I smile and turn my attention to Sadie. "Just moved to Chicago?"

"Moved back, actually. I was living in upstate New York for college but grew up in the northwest suburbs, but I'm staying at my brother's place here in the city to help him out before the school year starts." Sadie's eyes have a way of holding mine when she talks, and her voice is smooth and perfect. Angels must ask her for advice on how to speak.

"School year?" I question. They're both younger than Cole and me—my guess is they're mid-twenties, and we're pushing thirty-two. I wouldn't have guessed they were still in college, though.

Sadie swallows from her straw. "Mmm, yeah. I work at the public library up on the north side—well, I help organize the education and outreach programs there."

Ruby excuses herself for a moment to head to the ladies' room, but Sadie and I don't particularly notice Ruby's departure.

"Okay. So technically, I could call you a librarian? You probably have matching sweaters and glasses too." I flash my eyes at her, because something tells me that she's up for my dirty innuendo.

Her lips quirk as she tries to contain a grin. "Wow, a few minutes in and you take us there."

I lean into the table and let my eyes give her a once-over… *again*. "Are you complaining?" She doesn't answer, but I see the subtle shake of her head. "Enjoying a summer in the city? How is that going for you?"

She smiles. "So far okay, but it's only the beginning of June. Don't think I have enough data to make a conclusion."

I smirk at her reference. "Now you're going to tell me you're into math and finances."

"Absolutely not. I find it quite stuffy and boring."

My hand finds my heart. "Ow, that's a blow to my ego. Guess I'm stuffy and boring."

She bites the corner of her mouth. "I don't know. Are you?"

"Most would say the opposite actually."

Her brow raises and she seems intrigued. "Really? How so?"

I look at her and debate what to say, drinking from my glass. "I'll tell you another time. It isn't safe for the ears around here."

She enjoys my reply and coyly answers, "But maybe there isn't another time."

My eyes narrow as I study her and consider where to lead this conversation. "Well, considering you're staying in the city and I live in the city, then I would say we could make another time happen."

Now she blushes. A new record for me; she held off for so long.

She even has this soft gentle laugh to accompany her smile. "Is that how it pans out for you? Say a line like that and then have a woman at your beck and call?" Sadie is teasing me.

I sit back in my chair. "Wow, you really have an image of me that I'm not sure is in my favor."

"I only just met you," she counters as she watches her finger circling the rim of her glass.

"True. So, tell me about you. Is there a boyfriend waiting for you somewhere?"

Her eyes flick up to meet mine. "Nope. I'm going to take a wild guess that you're single, otherwise you wouldn't have asked."

I rest my head against my propped arm on the back of the chair. "Correct on all counts. My life is too chaotic at the moment."

"How so?" She seems genuinely interested.

I smile softly. "Work, family, and it seems there are single women walking around this city doing some damage to the male population."

She licks her lips and then nibbles her lip. She's drawing me in, and I think she knows it.

Sadie and I don't break eye contact as Ruby returns and settles into her seat.

"Did I miss anything exciting?" Ruby asks, looking between us.

My eyes can't seem to part from Sadie. "Your friend was just telling me about herself, but I didn't get further than she's single."

But I see out of the corner of my eye Ruby looking at Sadie. I know women enough to recognize Ruby is giving the you-are-in-trouble grin to Sadie, as she should.

Ruby turns her attention to me. "Well, Sadie likes cupcakes, walks, and loves puppies. She won a hula hoop competition too—"

"I did no such thing." Sadie shakes her head, then shrugs a shoulder. "It was once and, it was for charity."

I cross my arms and look at her with a partially gaped-open mouth and wide eyes. This is an interesting fact that my dick thoroughly enjoys.

"Sounds like you are the life of the party," I comment.

"Anyhow, enough about me. Logan is staying vague on details. I can't possibly say I've learned anything new about him." Sadie tilts her chin up at me.

Something tells me she could be a little vixen, and that gets me excited.

Before I can respond, Cole interrupts us by slapping a hand on my shoulder. "I think you ladies have dinner reservations, and your father wanted me to tell you that he will meet you inside. Hope Logan wasn't boring you two too much."

"Boring is debatable," Sadie answers, one-toned yet with a subtle grin on her face as she cocks her head to the side.

How have our eyes not blinked?

"Thanks for taking the edge off my father," Ruby mentions to Cole. "Now we can actually have a conversation sans business at dinner."

"Anytime," he answers, and I wonder if he notices that Ruby is giving him a fond look as we all stand.

"Well, you ladies have a good dinner. I recommend the lemon meringue pie, it's good," I suggest as we all begin to walk inside. Cole and Ruby walk ahead, and it gives me the opportunity to gently grab Sadie's arm.

She glances at her arm then angles her gaze up to me with a radiant look.

"I don't have a puppy, but there is a good cupcake place near my office if you ever want one?" I give her my best smooth grin that has often led me to success as I pull out a business card from my inner suit pocket.

The corners of her mouth tug. "Hmm, trying to watch my sugar intake, and I am quite busy next week."

I hand my card to her. "I can deliver the cupcake if it's easier."

She takes the card and glances at it then lets her index finger stroke the edge of the board. "This card is trouble, isn't it?" Her eyes glare at me.

My lips tilt up due to the tone of her answer. "I think you like that prospect."

She looks away as a soft smile forms, before returning her gaze to me, and she's looking at me with doubt now. "Didn't you say your life is kind of chaotic now?"

Well, that was a harsh reminder.

"Good point. But it won't always be chaotic. Do I count

on you to contact me or should I just ask for your number now?"

"Does this charm work on many women?" She sounds skeptical.

"So, I *am* charming?" I give her my best grin and don't get an answer, as everyone begins to say goodbye to one another. I'm wondering how I can see this woman again, but my brain reminds me that this weekend I have to collect my nephew.

As Cole and I are downstairs waiting for our cabs, I'm curious if I am destined for a few months of painful blue balls, because already my new life schedule is cockblocking me.

2

LOGAN

I t's Sunday, and I've picked up my nephew and his luggage. It was a full-on house move it seems. Already my penthouse is filled with an abundance of Legos and airplanes scattered across the floor. Not to mention, my nephew comes as a package deal with a hamster in a cage that is now stationed in the living room on my expensive cabinet. My place looks like a warzone, and it's only been six hours.

"What is all this crap?" I ask my sister via Facetime on my phone as I sit at my kitchen island.

"I made sure Mom packed everything. There should be bed linen and enough clothes. His lunchbox is in the green bag. Mom packed a bunch of stuff in the cooler bag for the next few days for his lunch, but then you're going to need to pack his lunches for later in the week." My sister is lying in bed with the sound of monitors beeping in the background. Her brown hair is in a giant nest on the top of her head, and she is wearing a sweatshirt that says, "Party of three," and she looks, well… exhausted.

"Okay, what about the afternoons? I have a hell of a week ahead, trying to close a deal with a client."

"Relax. The agency was able to find a nanny, and she will pick him up from summer camp at two pm and then take him to your place. They'll practice reading, and she will ensure he eats dinner, then wait until you get home. I haven't spoken to her yet—it was all arranged by the agency last-minute, since the original nanny cancelled, but a friend of mine knows her. Please be kind to her. She was recommended, and my friend claims she's like a supernanny or something—plus, she has a background in helping with dyslexia, and Mason really needs to work on his reading over the summer. She should be stopping by your place in like ten minutes to get the key… but maybe interrogate her a little for me. I mean, check that she's a suitable fit."

Looking over at my nephew, I see he's on his tablet, then look back at my phone screen. "Alright, will do. And how are you feeling?"

"Okay, I hope I make it to thirty-five weeks but grabbing a snack from the tray is too much." Zoe sighs and lets her head fall back onto the pillows.

"Let me send someone to bring you some normal food?" I offer for the fiftieth time. Our parents help her, but they can't do it full-time since they live out in the suburbs.

"Nah, maybe when the twins are born, I'll take you up on your offer for hired help."

My door buzzes, which means the doorman is letting me know someone is coming up. "Oh, seems like your nanny is right on time. Have to go."

"Please don't be an ass. We need her to make this all work, and Mason needs structure," she begs.

I grin at my phone. "Relax, I will be a perfect gentleman. You sent me an ugly-looking one, right? I mean, we won't have a problem then," I joke, but I *may* be serious.

My sister gives me an unamused look. "Actually, she is

kind of cute. Well, at least from the photo I saw in the file the agency sent. So, keep it locked up and do *not* sleep with her," she warns me with a pointed finger.

I walk toward the door. "I promise, best behavior. Bye," I quickly say and end the call before she can respond.

Heading to the door, I call out to my nephew, but his earphones are flattening his thick curly brown hair. Fine. It just means I can make this conversation with the nanny quick and to the point.

The nanny needs to know that I'm the boss and that we need to run a smooth ship. I have too many meetings to attend, and if all goes well, then in the coming weeks, I will have scored my biggest client to date.

Leaning against the inner pane of the door, I watch as the elevator doors open. I realize in this moment that I never asked for the name of the nanny. *My bad.*

My eyes draw a line up from the floor to the skinny-jeans-covered legs, up to a light blue t-shirt with some off-the-shoulder action happening, and as soon my eyes find her face, I know this is just crazy. Or bad. Or perfect luck.

"Sadie," I say with a grin forming across my face.

Her beautiful mouth opens, and the surprise on her face seems pleasant. "What are the chances you're waiting for a nanny?" She steps into the hall and stands still.

"I would say very high."

I should probably nix the idea of wanting to bang her into next year, but surely, it's okay if I keep that thought playing on a loop in my head?

My eyes assess the view, a damn fine view, as I cross my arms and casually lean against the door. "What are the chances you're waiting for the perfect boss?"

SADIE

Biting my lip, I glance away briefly before returning to look at the perfect image of a man in front of me.

This is a coincidence I didn't see coming, and I'm not sure why I have a wave of excitement running through me right now. Especially as this is a job to help me pay off student debt and tide me over until I start my new job, the one that my parents would consider the start of my career. But this doesn't feel like a job—suddenly this feels like an adventure that I'm embarking on.

That smug grin on his perfectly carved face has been in my head since the other day when we met, with a little stubble that would feel great nuzzling up my thigh. His deep blue eyes seem to be checking me out, I can't be imagining that.

Business Logan was sexy, but Casual Logan, with jeans and a white t-shirt is not exactly a bad look either. I didn't notice when he was in his suit, but I see it now—he has some amazing arm action happening. The wave of his brown hair is ruffled compared to the other day. He's sexy, slightly cocky, and way too confident. He is trouble, but the good kind of trouble, if there is such a thing.

Sadie, get some damn composure.

"Are you going to stand there or come in?" He is clearly amused by this change of events or the fact my mouth has gaped open like a Labrador waiting for a treat.

I only manage to nod my head in agreement as I follow him into his place. Right away, I notice how open and big his little palace in the sky is. Logan's place is modern with high ceilings and windows overlooking great views of the river downtown, and there's even a big balcony with table and chairs.

Following Logan, we enter his kitchen area filled with steel appliances. The whole place is open-plan, so I notice who I assume is Mason, who was mentioned in the file, sitting on the couch and oblivious that I arrived. Kids these days and technology.

Logan opens the fridge and disappears behind the fridge door. "Want something to drink?"

He re-emerges with a beer bottle in hand and indicates to me if I would like one.

I shake my head no, having decided I need a clear head for this conversation. I guess he has a child, which means there must be an ex in the picture.

Leaning against the kitchen counter, he pops open the beer bottle with a key that was in his pocket and takes a drink. "So, this is a coincidence." He grins.

I lean against the opposite counter. "I didn't know you have a child."

The corner of his mouth hitches up. "I don't." I'm really confused, and he must see that. "He's my nephew," Logan clarifies as he hops up on the counter to sit.

"Oh, sorry, I was given vague details by the agency."

Logan looks at me, puzzled. "I thought you work at the library as the hot librarian."

I smile that he remembers. "I do, starting in the academic year, and *not* as the hot librarian. Anyhow, I want to work a little in the summer."

"I thought you were helping your brother?" His gaze doesn't leave me as he drinks from his bottle and queries me.

"I am. I'm apartment sitting since he's too busy with his work outside the city, and he has a great apartment not far from here. Anything else you remember?" I raise a brow, amused.

Logan huffs a laugh to himself. "Yeah, something about hula hoops and bikinis."

My eyes shoot to him, and I hope my face remains a neutral color.

"You had no clue?" he asks.

I look around the room to avoid his gaze. "No clue. I mean, I've had contact with the agency, and the information was scarce other than the job is for a seven-year-old boy named Mason."

"So, I should probably brush you up on *that* situation." He sets his bottle down and indicates his head down the hall as he begins to walk, and I follow. Logan has that type of presence that just allows him to lead, and you respond without question.

We stop in front of a door that Logan opens, then he nudges my arm with his own to follow him into the room. He has some strong fingers that tug my arm, and I can only imagine what they're capable of. Somewhere deep within me is stirring at that thought.

Right away, I'm aware it's a bedroom—and *not* a child's room. For some reason, the thought that I'm in a bedroom with this man turns on a signal between my legs, and that should not be happening considering he's my new boss. My eyes are moving in all directions, as I don't know where to look.

The room is massive, but I see Logan now standing in the middle of the room in front of me with a hand on his hip. I can't help but notice the perfectly made bed with navy blue linen, and it's big, probably comfy too.

I wonder if he sleeps naked. I shake my head to bring me back to the moment.

"Mason is a great kid, I love my nephew. But truthfully, this arrangement for him to live with me couldn't have come at a worst time. I'm in over my head at work and need to close the deal of a lifetime within two weeks. Assuming you still want to help, then I really need this to go smoothly. Not just for me, but for Zoe, my sister. She will kill me if Mason seems unsettled, and I've already pissed her off enough for a lifetime."

"I can only imagine." I'm sarcastic, and I can see he enjoyed my remark by the way the corner of his mouth twists. I step closer to him out of instinct. "Where is she anyhow?"

Logan sighs as he brings a hand up to rub his forehead. "She is in the hospital, pregnant with twins. There's a complication, something with the placenta, so she has to be monitored. They hope to keep the babies in at least another few weeks. Obviously, Mason can't be at the hospital all the time, and it's the summer, so no school, and I agreed to have him stay here."

"Oh, I hope your sister is okay."

"Thanks. She'll probably call you tomorrow with a full rundown on what to do with Mason, but let's keep any interactions with Zoe pure rainbows. So even if Mason is acting like a little brat, which does happen—we lie. She doesn't need the stress, and Mason has no clue how serious it is that she rests," he explains as he walks to the floor-to-ceiling window to look out.

"Very clear."

He glances over his shoulder at me. "Ah, so you're still in and willing to do this?"

"Why not? Or do you think I'm not up to the job?" My brow furrows.

Logan leans against the window to face me, and that complacent grin comes back. "I think you are exactly who I want to do this job, but you do know that you may need to spend the night a few times." His tone is neutral.

I blink and try to contain an impartial face. "And? I assume you have a spare room."

My demeanor makes the corners of his mouth curve up again. "So, not a problem?" He cocks his head at me.

"Not a problem… I don't mean to pry, but Mason's father?" I bite my lip, slightly afraid I'm crossing the line.

"Not in the picture. The twins' father has only met Mason a handful of times, as he is overseas and obviously isn't around right now. My parents also help out from time to time, but they don't have the energy for Mason every day, plus his summer camp is here in the city and they live out in the suburbs."

I nod in understanding as my hands find my jeans pockets, and I can't help letting my eyes wander the room again. I'm slightly curious, slightly concerned that this is where Logan Jax probably has women coming in and out like a revolving door. I had Ruby fill me in on any details she may have known about Logan, and while she wasn't negative about him, she did point out the fact that he has a fan club in the city.

He steps away from the window. "Look, I know nothing about what you will do with Mason. I told Zoe to find a nanny and that I'd pay. She mentioned something about how he needs to practice reading. I know he had problems at school, but again, I'm clueless. His books are in one of his backpacks, along with a list from his school."

"Yeah, he has a special education teacher who assigned him some workbooks for the summer. That was in his file," I mention and admire the man in front of me who is 100% clueless like he says but seems to care about his role as uncle.

"I'll give you a credit card and you can use that for him and groceries. I most likely will be home after dinners. You cook?" he asks, skeptical, yet he has a suave grin as if he isn't asking for Mason's sake.

I lick my lips before biting the corner of my mouth. "I do… cook," I manage to answer, and our eyes meet.

He tilts his chin up. "Ah, good to know."

Our eyes settle and there's silence, but we both have wry smiles.

Clearing my throat, I let my fingers tap my jeans as my thumbs hang off my pockets. "So, if we're done talking about the things you didn't want Mason to hear then maybe… we could head out of your bedroom?" I give him an entertained look.

His tongue glides around his mouth and he purses his lips. "Sorry, didn't realize where we were."

"You don't sound convincing," I counter.

His grin turns wide. "You like it."

It's not that I *don't* like it.

He walks past me, causing me to get a whiff of his scent. It's subtle and reminds me of spring.

Heading back into the living room, Mason peers his head up like a chicken. "Who's she?" *Whoa*, the seven-year-old has some attitude in his voice.

Logan laughs under his breath as he goes to take the headphones off his nephew and encourages him to stand. "This is Sadie. She is going to pick you up from camp and stay with you until I'm home every night." He nudges the kid in my direction.

I lean down. "Hey, Mason, I'm Sadie."

"My mom says that you've been hired to take care of my uncle."

I chuckle at his comment and look up to Logan who is shaking his head.

"Why would you think that, buddy?" Logan asks as he places his hands on Mason's shoulders.

"Because Mommy says you need to be kept in line."

My eyes go wide as I look at Logan who is biting his inner cheek in delight.

"Aren't you a cute guy," I say to Mason and let my hand rustle his hair. He is quickly stealing the show, and that's hard to do with Logan Jax in the room.

I'm not oblivious to the fact that Logan has the sexy-bachelor persona going on. I've seen him now in a suit and in casual clothes—he's easy on the eyes. And maybe he has this slick way of communicating that some may see as arrogant yet charming.

It can also spell danger, and I am completely aware.

"This may be a long summer," Logan mentions to himself as he scratches the back of his neck.

Tell me about it.

I stand back to adult height as Mason goes to grab something from the kitchen cupboard.

"Anything else I should know?" I raise my shoulders to the direction of my ears as my hands find my back pockets out of nervous habit.

"My number."

My eyes flick up to meet his and, sure enough, that cocky satisfied grin is on his face.

"In case of emergency," he clarifies, with his eyes acting as some sort of lasers that are making me feel all types of warm.

"Right, but I think I already got your card with information." Again, I kill it at the pretend cool-and-confident persona. Still, I hand him my phone so he can type in his number, and he must also hit call, because I hear his phone vibrate in his pocket.

He passes my phone back and our fingers brush, which sends a tingle to parts of my body that my t-shirt choice will not protect me from.

Logan wiggles his own phone in his hand. "Look at that. Now I have *your* number."

"So you do. And the key?"

He walks to a drawer near the sink and grabs a key then hands it to me. "The cleaner comes on Mondays, so don't be surprised if she's here tomorrow. I should be home by eight, but it depends on a call I have with overseas clients."

"What is it you do again?" I wonder.

A half-smile forms on his face. "Stuffy data and financials." He's teasing me for what I said the other night, but then continues, "I manage a hedge fund."

"Can't say that is entirely interesting," I respond with some honesty, and he seems to enjoy that I'm not giving him a typical polite response, as his lips quirk.

"Uncle Logan, I'm hungry," Mason groans.

"I'll order pizza, okay, buddy?" Logan calls out to Mason who is now eating from a bag of goldfish crackers while he looks through the cupboards for more food.

"Well, I should go. I have the key and your number, plus I've seen your bedroom, so we're all set," I ramble and begin to walk, realizing I brought his bedroom back into the equation.

Logan leans against the counter, crosses his arms, and gives me a look that tells me this is really going to be a long freaking summer.

"Hey, most women can only check off one of those things you mentioned on your list. You're living the dream."

I look at him, taken back by his arrogance. "Definitely my cue to leave."

He propels himself off the counter as we walk towards the door. "I was joking with you; you know that, right?" His tone sounds sincere, and when I study his face, I can see that he appears genuine.

"It doesn't matter." I brush it off.

He opens the door for me and there is an awkward pause as neither one of us moves.

"So, I guess I will see you tomorrow, just text if you need anything."

I nod, very much aware that I need to get used to his piercing blue eyes landing on me. "Sure. Bye, Mason," I call back into the room. I will need to win him over tomorrow, as he is too occupied to even try now.

"No goodbye for me, your new boss?" Logan gives me a faux pained look.

I playfully shake my head as I bite my inner cheek. I will *not* flirt with my new boss.

"Bye, Logan." I walk away, determined to show I am unaffected.

But inside, I am very much feeling the opposite.

4

SADIE

Anxiously, I wait for the kiddos to appear from the end of their day at camp. Lined up with a bunch of moms and my guess a few other babysitters, I stand outside by the playground. It's a scorching-hot day; it's supposed to be warm all week. My phone vibrates in my jeans pocket, and I quickly pull it out to answer.

"Hi, it's Sadie."

"Oh, hi, it's Zoe, Mason's mom." She sounds quite cheerful.

"Hi, yeah, Logan mentioned you would call. How are you feeling?"

"Ugh, like a whale and an elephant morphed into one. Just wanted to check in to see if you had any questions? He'll most likely bite a little."

My eyebrows furrow, concerned. "Mason?"

Zoe laughs. "No, my brother. He can be a little impulsive sometimes, or just plain trouble. Just ignore him."

It makes me smile. "Oh… right. That I can do." *I think.*

"Mason normally needs a snack mid-afternoon, and he does his reading either before dinner or before bed."

"Yeah, Logan mentioned something about a backpack and all of Mason's books are in there."

"Oh, so he does listen." Zoe sounds impressed.

"We will all be fine, I promise."

"I'm sure. I'm more worried about my brother than Mason, actually. This situation really put a wrench in his lifestyle."

Now I nervously laugh, and she must have heard my *uh* sound.

She clarifies, "My older brother is a book of clichés. He works hard, like any corporate mogul would, is charismatic, and I am positive he only sends fruit baskets to women he sleeps with to end their trial run. He is the cliché bachelor, and now I throw a seven-year-old into his sphere. No more dates back at his place, you know?"

I adjust my neck, slightly uncomfortable with this conversation. Not because Logan's sister is the one telling me, but the context of what she's saying. A tinge of jealousy runs through me at the thought of him bringing dates back to his place, which is just borderline insanity.

Oh, right, she asked me a question.

"I guess maybe that is the case, I don't know. I only just met him."

"I know. Just, thanks for helping. I don't want to make Logan's life more complicated. He is already helping me above and beyond."

"It's no problem. Do you want me to call you when Mason is out?"

"No, that's okay. I'll call tonight. Have a good first day together." I can hear the smile in her voice.

"Okay. Well, we'll be in touch."

I hang up and put my phone in my bag. Just in time too, as a bunch of kids come running out. I wave to Mason to grab his attention, and he slowly walks my way with his backpack on and a cap on his head.

"Hey, Mason, remember me?"

"Yeah, you're the babysitter for my uncle."

Wow, they are all in it together, it seems—team tame Logan.

I chuckle. "That's me. Should we head back to your uncle's place to get a snack or want to have a snack at the playground?"

"I want to go swimming. There's a swimming pool on the roof of my uncle's building." He sounds amazed.

"Oh, that sounds fun. Maybe later in the week?"

"Fine." The disappointment is apparent.

We begin to walk down the street to grab a car that was arranged for us by Logan's assistant and head back to Logan's.

Half an hour later, I make Mason a snack of cheese and crackers. We then go for a walk to the nearby playground where I kick a ball around with him, then we head to the supermarket to stock up on supplies for dinner. After drawing together, I whip up a simple spaghetti Bolognese and decide I should check in with Logan. Pulling out my phone, I find his name. Tilting my head to the side, I change his name on my phone before texting him—I need to keep myself reminded.

> Hey! Pick-up went well, we went to the playground and now home. I spoke to your sister too.

OFF-LIMITS BOSS

Oh yeah? Don't believe a word she says.

> Oh, so I shouldn't think you're trouble?

???

> She has some theories.

> Care to explain?

I send him a winking emoji, knowing that little yellow head is a dangerous emoji to use.

> I should get back to your nephew. You probably have some stuffy numbers to tend to also.

I smile to myself.

> Probably, see you later.

Looking at Mason who arrived at the kitchen counter, I begin to serve him up some pasta.

"What's your favorite food, Mase?"

"Uhm, pizza, tacos, ice cream, the stuff Uncle Logan lets me have."

Of course, a seven-year-old would think Logan's child-care tactics are the best. "Your mom doesn't let you have that stuff?"

Mason leans over the counter and puts his hand around his mouth to loudly whisper. It's adorable. "Shh, we aren't supposed to let my mom know that Uncle Logan lets me eat the bad stuff."

"Your secret is safe with me," I promise in the same tone.

He is busy attacking his spaghetti by pouring more parmesan cheese on his plate, and my curiosity gets the best of me.

"Hey, Mase, do you see your uncle a lot?"

He nods his head up and down. "When my mom had a smaller belly, we all had dinner together every Sunday night."

I study his face. "Miss doing that? I'm sure your mom misses you a lot," I try to assure him. It's important he talks about his mother.

"I know, but she has to take care of my sisters."

"Sisters?"

"Yeah, the babies are girls."

I smile at him. "Ah, so you're going to be a big brother to sisters, that's special."

He slants a shoulder to his ear. "I'll just do what Uncle Logan does and take care of them the way he does for my mom."

That is a really sweet comment and doesn't help the sex-appeal factor of my off-limits boss.

I let a few seconds pass before continuing my quest. "And, Mase, is your uncle always alone at these Sunday dinners?"

I'm a horrible babysitter for sneaking that in.

His little brown eyes peer up at me. "Normally, yeah."

"Normally?"

"Sometimes his friend Cole comes with."

That's a relief.

"Okay, so after dinner, you'll take a shower, get your pajamas on, then we can read a book. Your choice. Sharks or bears."

"Sharks," he quickly answers.

"Good choice. I think you're going to the aquarium with your camp group; they have sharks there."

"Cool."

A few minutes later, he runs off and I clean up the counter, wondering if I should save a plate for Logan. I do, just in case.

My phone vibrates, and I look to see it's my best friend, Emily. Ruby, Emily, and I all went to the same high school together. Ruby left for boarding school halfway through, but Emily and I have remained close throughout the years. She went to Boston for college, and I went to upstate New York. We made it a point to always see one another when we could.

"Holding up?" she greets me via video call.

"Yeah, it's actually fun. I guess Logan will be home soon." I place my phone on speaker and prop it up against a jar so I can continue cleaning up.

"Right, and then do you go home or…?" she prompts me.

I roll my eyes. "Not going to happen," I remind her, as I already explained twice yesterday when we had a group chat with Ruby, and I told them about the coincidence of Logan being my new temporary boss.

"Come on, Sadie, didn't you mention before you knew he was your boss that you were both sending off some vibes when you met?"

"I insinuated no such thing," I correct her, even though I know it's a lie.

She laughs into the phone. "Right. And you aren't at all interested in discovering what he keeps in his bedroom drawer?"

My head bobbles, as I can't deny that is true.

"Look, he has a lot going on in his life," I explain. "He barely makes it home to say goodnight to his nephew. He doesn't have time for, well… *that*."

"He's a guy. He always has time for *that*."

"Yeah, and then it gets awkward between us and I have to face him for the next few weeks. It's a little risky."

"Or you just have a little fun and consequences be damned."

I mean, I could have a little fun. I've always only been with people I dated and thought for a millisecond that we could go somewhere in the future. But I think I like fun. It's just, I've never really met someone who seemed exciting enough to take a chance on only fun.

I shake my head to refocus. "Anyhow, I have to go check on Mason. When Logan gets home, I'll leave quickly."

"Why? Because you don't trust yourself around him? Good luck with that." She laughs before we end the call.

Luck is exactly what I need. It's been three months since I've had any action outside my vibrator, and before that it was only mediocre. Now I am spending most of my waking hours in Logan's home. The place smells of him, I've seen his bed, I got a glimpse of his shower that is the perfect size for two. Hell, the hallway closet even looks like an appealing place to experience receiving an orgasm or two. And soon, that walking piece of success and hotness will be striding in here for the evening. It will be this way every day for the next few weeks.

Yeah, luck is exactly what I need.

5

LOGAN

Leaning back in my chair behind my desk, I admire the view of the Loop with a sigh. For six weeks, I've been in the final negotiations with a company out in Seattle to bring their business to my portfolio so we can manage their investment portfolio. We have a two-week deadline to seal the deal. The project team is doing their best, and we are all working hard—but it may just come down to luck.

My phone vibrates on my desk, and I see it's Cole. I swipe to answer and leave the phone on the desk.

"Hey, man, what's up?"

Cole speaks on the other end, and from the sound of cars driving by in the background, it sounds like he's outside. It makes sense, as it's past dinner time and I'm still at the office. "Have you met the nanny yet?"

I laugh deeply because I know he is going to love the latest. "You mean Sadie?"

"What? As in the friend of Ruby's from the other night? She's the nanny?" He sounds surprised, as he should be.

"Yep."

"Small world."

"Tell me about it."

"This is perfect. You were checking her out, and now you'll see her every day. I give it a week tops before you mess that up."

"Whoa, thanks for your vote of confidence—and this isn't good news. I am on strict orders from my sister not to mess anything up for Mason, and she's right. Less chaos is the way to go."

"Do you really think you have the restraint?"

I've been questioning that. I hope for both my mental health and the restraint of my cock that today she isn't wearing anything light, baby pink or blue, or something angelic that gives off the image she is innocently sweet, because it only encourages me to want to ruin her for all other men.

An audible exhale escapes me. "Again, your vote of confidence is great," I say sarcastically.

"Isn't this whole situation only temporary? I mean, she won't be in the picture as the nanny forever, right?" Cole asks.

"Look, Cole, I should head out. I have a lot to do, and I need to get home on time now, since there's my nephew and a very hot nanny waiting for me." I crack a smile to myself.

Cole chuckles deeply on the other end. "Those are the words that many men want to say but only a few get to. Something tells me she is in trouble."

"Maybe just."

We hang up, and I have to think about it. Being attracted to the nanny probably isn't a smart move given the dynamics of this situation, but eventually Mason will be back with my sister and Sadie won't be the nanny. I mean, that's probably six weeks at best. In the meantime, I can work my charm on her and wear her down a little. There's no harm in that.

———

Opening the front door, I walk into my place, and I hear quiet except for the voice of Sadie encouraging Mason to read his book about sharks. I try to be silent as I head into the kitchen, and I can see they're sitting on the sofa.

"You got it. Are you getting tired? You read a lot." She smiles at Mason.

"Really?" he asks, surprised.

"Yeah, we read a whole chapter. I don't even read chapters of books in one day." Sadie is being a bit overdramatic when she says that, but I don't think Mason picks up on it.

"It sounded good, kiddo," I say to announce my arrival.

Both Sadie and Mason turn their heads to look at me. My nephew jumps up and runs over for a hug. Sadie nibbles her bottom lip, and truthfully, it flashes in my head what it could be like if she does that while lying on my bed, especially since she's wearing a tank top that accentuates her assets, and I'll be damned, but they look quite firm too.

"Didn't hear you come in," Sadie mentions, and her mouth tugs into a smile as she tucks hair behind her ear.

"Didn't think I should interrupt." I hand Mason my phone after unlocking it. "Here you go, your mom is expecting a call from you now." Mason runs off to his room.

My focus returns to Sadie who is straightening out the books on the coffee table.

"You're back earlier than I expected. He had dinner already, and Mason's already in his pajamas, so you're good to go with bedtime."

I loosen my tie and begin to work the top buttons loose. "Thanks. It helps a lot."

"Well, I'll let you guys have your evening, and I'm going to head off." She moves toward her bag.

"*Or* you could stay and have a glass of wine with me. I normally have a drink after work. Mason will head to bed after he speaks with my sister." I'm already walking to the wine fridge to survey the options.

"*Yeah*. Maybe I'll take a raincheck." I look up and see her lips roll into her mouth, and she appears slightly thrown off.

I have to subtly smile. "Come on, I should probably get to know the woman who is going to be in my house more than I am." I mean, there is some truth to that.

"I guess… *one* drink will be okay," she hesitantly agrees.

"Good. Give me a few minutes to change and tuck Mason in." I eye her as I gently knock on the counter before I leave. I continue to work the buttons of my shirt then turn around as I'm halfway toward the hall. "Help yourself, pick whatever bottle you want."

Yeah, I may have purposely turned around to give her a glimpse of my bare chest and stomach. Her parted mouth tells me she approves.

After changing into jeans and a black t-shirt, getting Mason into bed, and returning to the kitchen, I'm surprised to find that Sadie actually waited. It took twenty minutes at least.

She's reading what looks like cue cards as she leans over the counter, and her head turns up to me when I enter the space, a gentle smile forming on her face. "Everything okay with Mason?"

I take a look at the bottle she picked—a good choice, a crisp white.

"Yeah, he had a good time today. Don't know if it's the science camp or if you took top spot today, but it's close." I grab the wine opener and open the bottle as she watches. The sound of the popping cork breaks the unusual tension in the air.

I'm smart enough to know that it's probably the vibe of a man who has no problem flirting with the nanny, and the nanny who is unsure how to handle me but isn't complaining.

"Fun reading?"

She chortles. "You mean your sister's instruction cards that she left? Yeah, sure."

"Instruction cards?" I'm puzzled.

"Yeah, there's a card for everything. Recipes for dinner, reading checklist, snack ideas, laundry instructions, *and* how to put you in time-out." She says it as straight-toned as can be.

"Oh yeah?" I grin proudly.

She softly shakes her head. "No, but I feel like there should be instructions for that."

I like how this woman can rile me so naturally.

After pouring our glasses, we both walk to the sofa and have a seat. I can't help noticing that she sits a safe distance from me.

"Do you always work twelve hours a day?" she asks as she takes a sip of her wine and leans against the back of the sofa, tucking her knees under her on the cushion.

There is something really hot about a woman who walks around barefoot in skinny jeans and getting comfortable on my sofa.

"At least. Some days the office turns into dinners and turns to drinks. It can be a bit grueling," I admit.

"Sounds horrible, to be honest."

"How about you? Why are you doing the nanny thing?" I'm very curious how this puzzle piece fits into her story.

She smiles to herself. "Like I said, I'll start at the library in August. I just graduated with my master's degree actually, but I'm already two years behind in the professional world since college took longer."

"Why is that?"

She finishes her sip of wine. "I got shingles my sopho-more year of college and I ended up missing too many classes, so I had to repeat the year. Wasn't ideal, but at least I got better."

"Ouch, that isn't fun, but understandable why it took you more time."

"I wouldn't know what to do if I wasn't working for these few months."

"Travel, party, relax, the options are endless…" I list.

"Maybe. I was lucky that my parents paid for my under-grad, and I got a scholarship to cover my master's degree, but only partially. So, I want to pay that off in the next year. Then I can live debt-free." She says it so casually, unaware that not many people her age makes such sound financial decisions.

I have to admire that, and she must notice that I'm looking at her extra intently.

She shrugs a shoulder. "What? Not everyone lives like you."

I smile, amused. "That's what you think?"

She bounces a shoulder, unsure.

"Actually, my parents do alright, but they cut me off when I decided to take a break from college and travel. So, I ended up paying for part of my college too, but I just got lucky career-wise."

"Really lucky," she notes.

"Can't complain. But I'm happy to be in this situation."

"Right." It comes out long and distant from Sadie.

I feel like I hit chord or something. "Something you want to share?"

Sadie chews on the tip of her thumb as she debates what to say. "Your sister mentioned…" She smiles to herself.

"Go on," I encourage.

"She mentioned that you are the cliché successful bachelor."

I shake my head, entertained. "That's what my sister tells you when she calls to discuss her son?"

Sadie grins, clearly amused. "I mean, we did talk about Mason, don't worry."

"She's my twin, you know, I'm older by three minutes."

"Really?" Sadie says, intrigued. "Ah, that's why she called you her older brother. I guess twins run in the family then?" She drinks another sip of her wine.

"Guess so. You? You mentioned a brother?"

"An older brother, Wes. He lives in Detroit and has a whole successful entrepreneur thing happening. He still comes back to Chicago a lot, so he has a place here too. I see him a few times a year."

"You close?"

"Not like you and Zoe, but we are in contact with one another. Not exactly on a daily basis, but once a week maybe. He seems busy with his life, but I know if I need something he's only a call away. He's in Miami now for a few weeks for work."

"Miami is good, I prefer the Keys, though."

"Me too. I love Key West and the middle Keys. Do you travel a lot for work?"

I top up my wine and lean back into the couch. "Yeah, but the next two months I have to cut all of that down, obviously."

She gives me a sympathetic look. "It's really special, what you're doing."

"Not like I'm doing a lot. In the end, I see him at bedtime and breakfast."

She touches my arm. "Don't cut yourself short. You're doing a lot."

Her fingers are delicate, yet I love the tips of her fingers resting on my arm.

I adjust my body to angle more in her direction. "What are the plans for the week?"

"Mason wants to go swimming, is that okay?"

"Yeah, for sure. Just ask downstairs at the front desk and they'll show you where everything is. He's an okay swimmer—"

"Oh, I'll swim with him, no problem. It's supposed to be in the high eighties all week anyhow."

The image of Sadie in a bikini flashes into my head, and I'm seriously considering taking vacation hours off to witness this.

I only manage to nod in agreement before moving us swiftly on. "Would it be okay if you bring him to the hospital later in the week to visit Zoe?"

"Absolutely, just tell me when and where. He mentioned they're girls, the twins."

"Yeah, they are. Scares me that the world will get two mini Zoes; I can barely handle one." I let the back of my fingers glide along my upper lip as I think about that fact.

"Have you always been close with your sister? They say it's a special twin bond, right?"

"We've always been close. We've had maybe one big argument in our whole lives. Plus, she uses space at my office for her freelance editing work. I guess the strength of a twin bond is true."

I take the bottle of wine and pour more into her glass. Our conversation is flowing; it's easy, I've talked to her more about simple life things than I do with most.

"Twin babies are a lot to handle. She's very brave for doing it alone, and it's amazing too."

"Yeah, well, Mason's father was never in the picture. My

sister has a knack for finding complicated guys. The twins' father is overseas in the military and is so new to her life that I don't know what will happen there. Mason will stay with me the first few weeks after the twins arrive, so my sister can find a rhythm. We'll need to find a lot of things for him to do. His summer camp is only a few weeks more."

This whole explanation has me downing my wine in one go. Sadie firms her grip around my arm, and it's so incredibly calming.

"It's fine, there is so much to do with a kid his age during the summer," she tries to reassure me. "Will you be able to take any time off?"

"Depends. At the end of the day, I head the company, so I can bend the rules." I throw on a slightly cocky grin as I kind of want to impress her, which is insane because I know she already knows this about me.

She removes her hand from my arm which is kind of sad, but her cheeks raise as she tries not to let her grin form, and I like that.

"By the way…" She looks into her wine glass and almost blushes. "You mentioned the night we met about this cupcake place. Could you send me the name?"

"Ah, you really do like cupcakes. Ruby's facts are correct." I grin because that very much means another fact is accurate. "So, hula hoop champion in a bikini…"

Her face turns red, and she looks away as she finishes her own glass of wine. "I never mentioned a bikini, but yes. It was for charity, raising money for breast cancer awareness."

"Good cause," I quickly mention, but press on. "Remember any moves?"

"Maybe, but I reserve that for special audiences." She is absolutely flirting.

"Oh yeah? How do I get an invite?" I say casually as I tip

the wine bottle to my glass, but it's empty. "I'll go get another bottle."

"Absolutely not." Her palm flies up. "No. I mean, no… I'm done. I should get home. It's getting late, and this conversation is seriously dragging us into a corner." Her face is entertained as she gets up to stand and walks back to the kitchen, and I follow her.

"Corners can be good for some things," I mention as she sets her empty wine glass on the counter.

She grabs her bag with a wry smile set on her face. "I'm sure, but anyways, Mason's lunch is in the fridge and an extra snack. Oh, and there's a plate of food for you. I didn't know if you would eat or not, so I made extra," she rambles, and I'm also very pleased to hear that a woman cooked in my kitchen and there is homestyle food waiting for me in the fridge.

"We could have had dinner together? Didn't realize that was an option." I frown at that missed opportunity.

"I ate with Mason, so no. Nope. Not an option," Sadie replies as she walks toward the door.

"Wait." I grab her arm. We both look at my hand on her skin, and it would be so easy for me to tug her to me and kiss her senseless, but something tells me that's not the right move now. I look down at her. "Let me arrange for someone to take you home."

"It's okay. I'm only a few blocks away actually, in the Benton building."

"Ooh, that's swanky."

"Yeah, my brother does quite well, but really, it's fine, the walk," she notes.

A wave of protectiveness flows through me.

"We're not going to argue this. I'll have Jimmy at the

door arrange for you to get home. Every night, okay. You sure as hell are not walking alone at night."

She nods as our eyes hold. "Okay."

"Text me when you get home?"

She nods again, and only then do I realize I haven't let her arm go. I look down and let her arm free.

"Night, Logan." A gentle smile forms on her soft face. My name coming out of her mouth is sweet music to my ears. It's a perfect sound, and she should say it more often.

Just like her name that rolls perfectly off my lips. "Night, Sadie Bay."

She heads off to the elevator, and I watch every step. Our eyes are glued until the closing doors break our gaze. I smile to myself as I pull up my phone and call downstairs to ensure she gets home.

Fifteen minutes later, I'm lying in bed reading the overseas markets that just opened, and a message comes in.

SADIE

Home. Guess I'll see you tomorrow.

You'll see me every day.

Seems so.

Tomorrow, a bottle of red?

Sounds tempting, but I can't. I have plans.

Oh yeah, what a 24-year-old would do on a normal night.

Yeah, because you are so ancient.

She inserts a thinking emoji.

I'm 32, wiser than you.

Debatable.

Do I need to get home tomorrow on time so you can get to your appointment?

No, it's okay. It's not that kind of date. Night night.

Fuck, is she going on a date? Surely, she's going to knitting club or some gathering, whatever is hip these days. Can't say I'm thrilled with the idea of her going on a date with someone. Admittedly, even though I don't do relationships, I'm like a dog that doesn't share a bone.

And call me selfish, but I sure as hell will make sure that's not going to happen.

SADIE

Floating on the lime-green foam pool noodle, I watch Mason collect his rings and bring them to the steps of the pool before throwing the toys again and repeating the same exercise for the twentieth time. The sun is strong today and skies pure blue. Thank goodness I'm not scared of heights, because a pool on a roof of a tall building in downtown Chicago is not for the faint-hearted; it feels like we're dangling in the sky, with tiny cars and people way down below.

There's an older lady swimming her very slow laps, but for the most part we're alone. I can imagine not many families live in the building, and it is four pm on a Tuesday, so most are still at work. The sound of the toys flopping into the water merges with the faint sounds of the city, and it's quite relaxing.

"Should we head back inside soon? Make dinner?" I suggest.

"I'm not hungry. Can we stay out here?" Mason protests as he swims back to the steps.

"A little bit more, okay?"

"Uncle Logan!" Mason's smile grows wide as he looks at someone behind me.

I bounce slightly on my floaty noodle to get a better view. *How is that man not melting under this sun?*

Logan walks our way with swagger, his suit jacket slung over his shoulder, balancing on his finger. He ditched the tie at some point today, and a few loose buttons give me a glimpse of his chest with a few curly hairs. Sunglasses cover his perfect baby blues and make it impossible for me to grasp what he's staring at, but that sly grin gives me an idea. Logan sits on the edge of a lounger near us.

"Thought I would duck out of the office early to check on you guys," he mentions.

Mason has a huge grin as he waves a hand to encourage Logan to watch him as he throws his toys then swims to them. Logan looks in Mason's direction.

In the meantime, I swim toward the stairs and ditch the floaty that I was hanging off. I am completely aware that in a mere second I will need to walk up the steps of the pool in my black bikini and that I have an audience of one. And when Logan moves his sunglasses up to rest on his head, I now know his eyes are blazing with curiosity and satisfaction that he gets to watch, as proven by that half-grin forming on his perfectly carved face.

There are definitely flutters in my chest as I take the steps. And okay, I *may* ensure I sway my hips accordingly. As I walk toward my towel, the man of the hour quickly moves in front of me to grab the towel and hands it to me.

Our eyes meet and his bottom lip is hanging low. Truthfully, my mouth is parted from the idea that he's enjoying looking at me.

"Let me help you with that," he suggests as he holds the towel out wide.

"I think I can manage." I smirk.

"But I like it better if I can offer my services."

My chin tilts up. "Adding pool boy to your resume?"

He brings the towel behind me, and as he wraps, he encourages me to step closer to him. He closes the space between us, and my entire body reacts. Little goosebumps form on my skin and my nipples peak. His touch alone as he rubs the towel over my shoulders sends a desperate wave of want through me.

"Do you always wear a next-to-nothing bikini when babysitting?" he whispers into my ear. His tone, I can't figure it out. Is he teasing or is he telling me off? It's too sexy, it's almost wicked.

"Is there a problem?" I cock my head to the side.

A devilish grin spreads across his face before he leans again into my air and his breath tingles the skin of my neck. "Absolutely not; I encourage this for the rest of the summer."

In a way it makes me feel powerful that I have this ability to make him flirt with me.

I clear my throat and step back. "Come on, Mason, let's head back inside. Your uncle is feeling a little warm out here." I flash Logan a cheeky grin.

Five minutes later, we're back in Logan's penthouse. His gaze didn't leave me in the elevator, and I made sure to avoid his look, but I felt it on me. I set the shower on for Mason then left him with the door partly cracked. Heading to the kitchen, I see Logan is sitting on the kitchen counter with a look that tells me the next few minutes may be pure hell.

Pure hell for *me*—because I can't do the things that have floated into my mind. Like rip his shirt open to stare aimlessly at his chest, kiss his mouth, and let my fingers get entangled in his wave of hair.

I've known this man for a few days, and he has tapped

into something inside me that wants to be unleashed. It's the side of me that can be wild but has never had someone to be that way with. The guys I've been with were, well… lacking skill.

Taking a deep breath, I tighten the knot of the towel around my body and try to avoid him by heading toward the fridge to grab ingredients for dinner, but I stop in my tracks when I notice Logan is letting his fingers tap a white box.

"Thought you may want a cupcake." He doesn't blink, and the smirk on his face feels like he knows he's just gained points with me.

"You ditched work *and* got cupcakes?" I'm surprised by these two facts.

He shrugs a shoulder. "My assistant got the cupcakes, and I had the doorman bring them up while I went to find you and Mason at the pool."

Stepping closer to him, I tug the box away from his fingers that look like perfect little instruments of pleasure.

Opening the box, I'm impressed. They look delicious, a mixture of flavors and sprinkles. Cupcakes are a secret key to my heart too.

Closing the box and sliding it away from me, my eyes meet Logan's, and my mouth cracks a smile. "That is sweet of you. I'm sure Mason will love one after dinner."

"You should take them home; it'll be our secret. The kid never needs to know. They're for you."

I scoff. "No way. If he finds out, then I become the evil babysitter. Not going to chance that. We can share. Plus, I'm not going to eat a dozen cupcakes by myself."

"Guess you'll have to stay for dinner and dessert then," he encourages.

"I guess I could stay a little, but not too late."

"Right. You have that date." It comes out neutral.

It makes me smile to myself, because maybe, just maybe, things are beginning to make sense. He is either being polite and ensuring I get to my thing on time, or he is playing a game and trying to prevent me from going. I'm smart.

"I do." I play coy. "Anyhow, I'll check on Mason and quickly change, then figure out dinner."

"It's okay, I'll order Chinese. Take your time getting ready."

"Are you sure? I might take a quick shower then."

His eyebrows heighten and he scratches his cheek as he struggles to contain a mischievous look. "Feel free to use my shower, the shower in the guest room is getting fixed tomorrow. Anyway, my shower is made for two people, but you're going to have to settle for one, as I need to hang with my nephew."

I roll my eyes as I begin to walk away. "How thoughtful of you," I joke.

The next ten minutes, I use his bathroom to change and take a quick shower.

A horrible plan. Horrendous.

First, he only has men's soap, and it smells intense and fragrant, but the idea of being surrounded by his scent all night and getting it on my sheets when I sleep later is too good.

Then there is the problem that yes, his shower is meant for two, and damn it if that thought isn't stuck playing on a loop in my head. My eyes close as the water falls, and I imagine Logan behind me. It would be every bit as dirty as the idea that probably already exists in his head.

Finally, I groan because I can't be imagining this. He's flirting, I'm flirting, and there is chemistry. It's the type of energy that doesn't pass by often, you don't have that click with many.

I shake off that thought as I rinse the soap off. He's off limits, I need to remember that. Most definitely, he isn't a long-term kind of guy either, he would eventually get bored of me. I know the type, a man with zero regard of how it all ends. Nope. Kissing him would be a horrible idea.

How awkward it would be if I acted on this attraction then had to face him the next day when he arrived home in a suit with five-o'clock shadow. He doesn't seem like someone who is looking for a committed relationship, and I'm still undecided if I can handle no-strings-attached with anyone.

I sigh as I pop out of the shower, grab a towel, and in five minutes have myself in jeans and an off-the-shoulder t-shirt with sandals—my signature summer casual look.

Returning to the kitchen, I eye Logan and Mason sitting at the counter looking in the cupcake box.

"Have you picked out which one you want?" I ask Mason.

"Chocolate with sprinkles." Mason has a goofy look.

"Dinner will be here soon, but you know, I would think your date could spring for a decent dinner." He is surely riling me.

My hands find my back pockets and my shoulder rises up. "Maybe I just wanted to skip to drinks."

Logan quickly grabs the tablet from the counter and hands it to Mason. "Why don't you go sit in the living room, maybe put your headphones on," he encourages Mason, with his eyes never leaving mine, and Mason quickly scurries off.

"Now Sadie, that could give a guy the wrong impression. Especially on a first date—or is it not the first date?" It's almost as if he's giving me a lecture, and I love this interaction with him.

"Not the first date." I say it simply to see if his face changes.

Logan slides off the kitchen stool and glides a few steps around the counter into my bubble. He is clearly affected.

"Should I be worried?" He gives me an inquisitive look as he stops short of being too close for comfort.

I smile and lick my lips. "Since when did you become my chaperone?"

"I'm not, I'm your boss." A subtle smile forms on his mouth.

"Exactly," I volley.

He steps closer to me, but I just clear my throat and turn my back to him and step away, as we need a little space.

Glancing behind me, I see his face has a hardened look; he isn't impressed with my tactics.

I throw him a bone. "You never asked me what kind of date. You just assumed I'm meeting a guy."

His eyes go wide. "You're not?"

I can't help it; I enjoy toying with him, the way he does to me. Turning to him, I step closer and place my hand on the counter next to his arm, barely grazing his hand. He looks down to my hand then back up at my eyes.

"It's not that kind of date. I have a video call with a woman—"

"You better explain faster because already this is planting ideas in my head that are getting kind of wild."

I chortle. "What? A video call with a forty-year-old cat lady who is helping me with a research paper that I want to submit for publication?" I watch his brain connect the dots.

He laughs to himself. "That's your big date?"

"Yeah. I'll pour myself a nice glass of Shiraz as we talk about holistic approaches to helping children with ADHD."

His hands rake through his hair before going down the back of his neck, and he seems slightly disgruntled.

"This is a relief. I can't have my nanny on dates with random guys now, can I?"

"Are you going to keep calling me *your* nanny?" My hands find my hips.

He tilts his head to the side and his upper lip twitches. "Yeah, I think I am."

Before I can respond, the phone rings, and he answers. It seems to be the downstairs desk telling him the food has arrived. Our conversation needs to end due to logistics for dinner.

The next few minutes, I get plates and we unpack the boxes of Chinese food. We're all sitting at the dining table with the evening sun off to the west, and the view is so perfectly crystal clear that you could see out into the suburbs.

"When will I see Mom?" Mason asks.

"Later this week, then you're staying with Grandma and Grandpa for the weekend," Logan tells him as he spoons out more rice from the box.

"No, I want to stay here. Can we go to a baseball game like last time?" Mason tries his luck.

"Next week maybe. I can't this weekend," Logan explains.

"Big plans?" It shoots from my mouth out of curiosity and because I feel a nervous pit in my stomach that he's seeing a woman. *Those* kinds of plans.

Logan shoots me a daggered look. "Yeah, actually, a date with a 50-year-old guy from Seattle whose company I need in my portfolio. A solid glass of Chardonnay will be present."

I can't help but let a subtle smile show as our eyes catch. Turning my attention to Mason, I suggest, "How about we draw a picture or something to bring to your mom when we visit? Or maybe we can bake cookies?"

He nods his head. "She loves Skittle cookies."

"Skittle cookies?"

Logan laughs. "I think it's a pregnancy thing. Basically, chocolate chip cookies, but instead of chocolate chips, they're Skittles. Can't say I'm a fan."

"Okay. Well, that should be easy to make." Looking at my phone, I realize I need to get moving. "I'll see you tomorrow, Mase, I need to head out. Your uncle will read with you tonight, and you still have one page to do from your letter book."

He nods again as I get up from my chair.

"I'll be right back, kid," Logan tells Mason, and it seems he is following me to the door.

I grab my backpack from the floor. Logan is already leaning against the open door like a model and a man who only knows how to stand with confidence. "You didn't take a cupcake." He sounds disappointed.

"I'll have one tomorrow. I'm here almost every day, remember?"

"How could I ever forget?" His tone is soft and almost as if he's letting a thought escape.

"Well, goodnight, Logan."

"Night, Sadie Bay. You know the drill, text me when you get home. The front desk will make sure you have a ride."

"Thanks. Have a good night."

———

I HEAD OFF, and when I get home, I text Logan. After pouring a glass of wine, I speak with Carol via video chat as we go over a chapter of my paper about group programs between dieticians and parents with kids who have ADHD that I'm hoping to submit to an academic publication. She contributed to the research, so it makes sense. It's almost eleven when we finish our two-hour call.

As I get comfortable in my bed, wearing only underwear and a loose tank, my nose and lady parts recognize the familiar smell of Logan. Suddenly an overbearing thought and urge comes to me.

The moment my fingers hit my phone screen, I know I am playing with fire. Even after a few seconds of hesitation, I don't last and type away.

> Thanks for letting me use your shower. I now smell like you, and it's kind of infuriating.

It doesn't take long for the dots on the screen to move, which means he's up, and my guess is most likely in bed.

OFF-LIMITS BOSS

> Why infuriating? Can't handle being reminded of me? And no problem, use the shower anytime. Whether I am present or not.

He inserts a winking emoji.

> Me: Why would you be present?

> In case you need help.

> Me: Now, now, that's not very wise with your nephew running around.

> Ah, so you would consider if we were alone?

My entire body burns with heat as I blush to myself, and my hand can't help but migrate south to toy with the edges of my panties. I'm trying to type one-handed with the fingers of my other hand, but it's not my strong hand—I need that for the more important task.

I mean, if you're offering your services.

I insert an emoji with shrugging shoulders.

What services would you be interested in?

I debate how honest to be or if I should really cross this line. He is clearly giving me an all-clear signal, but I am well-attuned to the fact he has unexpectedly become temporary guardian to a seven-year-old and he's trying to focus on that situation.

…But it's only text.

No!

Maybe we'll discuss that another day.
Goodnight.

Leaving me hanging?

My mouth opens, and I wonder if it's the goddamn truth.

Were you holding onto something?

I smile to myself, proud of my comeback.

Maybe another day we'll discuss. Night,
nanny.

With the thought of that prospect, I let loose and take myself to the edge and over, hoping this fantasy doesn't just stay in my head.

7

LOGAN

My pen crashes against the back of my office door as I curse out an F-bomb that is normally reserved for more pleasurable experiences. This is not one of those times. For three hours solid, I've been on a call with William Vey who is dangling this financial portfolio like a carrot in front of me. The signs are there that it's all a go, but he isn't committing.

Jen, my assistant, jumps, slightly startled, and she corrects her glasses on her nose. She's been here for years so she's used to my outbursts.

"Shall I ask the trading team to stay and re-crunch numbers?"

I huff as I twirl on my chair behind my desk. "Nah, it's okay. I'll look into it personally. This weekend, only the best if William is still visiting. Room at the Ritz, dinner at the Grand, and make sure he has one of those architecture cruises in the morning. We don't spare any expenses on this one."

"All arranged already. Cole is also here for lunch, and the deli is delivering in five minutes. Shall I call the nanny to let her know you'll be late?" Jen is scribbling on her pad of paper.

"No, it's okay. I'll contact her." The thought of that makes my lips tug. Something enjoyable today at last.

Jen disappears, and I grab my phone that is lying on my desk. Swiping the screen, my fingers find Sadie's name, and I open our messages. I'm reminded of last night's zinger of a conversation that sent me to a happy place with my hand.

I type:

> Everything good today? Hate to do this, but I'm going to be late tonight.

SADIE

> I don't know, I haven't picked Mason up yet. It's not 2pm yet.

> And again, is everything good today?

> Can't complain. You?

> I've had better days

> How late is late tonight?

> Maybe nine? Is that a problem or have another research date?

> No. I have hula hoop class, but I guess I can miss it.

I'm staring at my phone, very happy that I told my assistant to leave the communication with the nanny to me. How am I supposed to eat lunch now with a hard-on forming? I know she's messing with me, but still.

> Oh funny. Do you listen to Doo-wop while you move?

Doo-wop? Guess you're older than I thought.

Yeah, so you should listen. I have some smart ideas.

Such as?

Oh, look at that, the time flew by and I have to get to a meeting. Talk later.

Cole comes walking in. The guy's presence just energizes the office. The interns are probably fanning themselves with him around. He stops by a lot too, especially since I hired his sister recently, so he swings by to take her to lunch.

"Look at that smile on your face. You getting some action?" Cole greets me as he finds my sofa and lies down, as if he's the one who owns the place.

"Is that all you think about these days?" I stop staring at my phone and slide it away to the side of the desk.

"No, but I want to know if you managed to survive your needed-to-leave-the-office-early-yesterday-to-see-Sadie-in-a-bikini scenario." He gives me a knowing look, as I called him on my way home yesterday, and within three seconds, he had called me on my play.

"Can't say I was complaining, that's for sure. Survived, too. I mean, it's just harmless flirting, and it turns out she didn't have a date-date," I explain.

Cole brings an arm behind his head as he stares at the ceiling. "Ah, so she is very much on the market. I don't see the big deal, just go for it."

I get up from my chair and walk to the front of my desk where I perch on the edge. "But I probably shouldn't add any more complications to my sister's life right now; did that once already. Plus, Mason would just get confused. He's had a hard enough year as it is. Mason hated school, then found out he would be sharing the spotlight with not one but two babies, and now he's stuck with me for the summer."

"Stuck with you *and* the nanny," Cole corrects me. "Who's to say that when Mason goes to bed you don't enjoy another glass of wine with Sadie and see where the night goes?"

"Except Sadie won't be quiet enough for what I have planned for her." I smirk because I can be a dick sometimes. "Besides, she's easy to talk to, has a sense of humor, and she can dish out what I give in return. I should probably not mess that up." I scratch my chin, because it's been a long time since I've had a woman around who I could also consider friendship material.

"Fine, but maybe you can have both. You're not the first guy to screw his nanny. Some even end up marrying their nanny. You would be a perfect cliché."

I walk over to the door as I speak. "Thanks. Exactly what I want to be," I joke as I take the food from Jen's hands to help her as she enters my office.

"Anything else you need? Oh, I booked a box at Wrigley for next week for Mason. Does the nanny come with to the baseball game?" she wonders.

Cole who is walking toward my table gives me a funny look. "Oh, I am sure she will be coming."

My pointed look lands on Cole before focusing on Jen. "Yeah, that's probably easiest. Sadie can meet me there with Mason."

"Ah, so you can be chaperoned by the kid for your date with her," Cole mentions as he pops a French fry into his mouth.

Jen's face lights up. "Are you dating the nanny?"

Here. We. Go.

"Nope, not dating the nanny."

"Oh? But you had me get cupcakes yesterday, and you wanted to speak to her today so I just thou—"

I cut her off. "Thanks for arranging lunch. We'll chat at the two-o'clock meeting." I usher Jen out.

"Okay, but let me know when I need to send a fruit basket," Jen offers.

"Not needed." I close the door behind her.

Jen has sent a lot of fruit baskets over the years, always for the same reason—to break up a good run at some fun or to steer a woman away from me and stop their dreams of something serious happening with a diplomatic thank-you card. Oranges with a few bananas thrown in for a little pop in color.

Turning my attention, I see Cole with his feet on my very expensive table and his arms crossed as he leans back in my chair.

"Now, this is something, if she isn't going to get fruit from you. You only give baskets to the ones who have no chance. Sounds like Sadie is on a higher pedestal."

"Maybe. Just maybe." Why does that even cross my mind?

———

By the time I finish looking at the financials for the fifth time, it's near ten pm. Shit, I really am late. I completely missed seeing Mason, and this isn't exactly fair to Sadie. Quickly, I shoot off a text to her.

> So sorry, lost track of time. Coming home now.

SADIE

No worries. Found Peaky Blinders on your
TV after getting Mason to sleep.

You're a Peaky Blinders fan?

Yes, but probably for different reasons than
you. Something tells me you don't watch it
for the hot actor.

True. Mason is out like a light?

I mean, just in case. It *could* be good if he is sound asleep
and out of the way.

Yeah, he was exhausted from camp, and
then we made cookies for Zoe.

Huh, there are homemade cookies at home. That's new
for me.

Okay, see you soon.

Except I don't see her soon. Nighttime road work can be a
killer, and I get stuck on a one-way route diversion on
Michigan Avenue, and it's eleven by the time I make it home.
When I walk into my penthouse, I smell the cookies right
away, and they smell good. As soon as I arrive in the living
room, I slow my pace as I walk toward the sofa with a smile
spreading.

Sadie fell asleep with the television softly on and a book
laid out on her chest. She's lying on the sofa with a hand near
her forehead, and she is gorgeous. A loose t-shirt falling off
her shoulders and jean shorts showing off her legs make this
scene borderline breathtaking.

I don't want to wake her. The normal thing to do would

be to grab a blanket and let her sleep on the couch, but that has to be uncomfortable.

Kneeling, I remove the book off her body—a book on diet and early childhood development. This woman isn't just looks; she has a brain too. Admiring the view a few seconds longer than I need to, I let the back of my finger brush along her cheek gently to wake her.

She's warm, she's soft, she smells of vanilla, and something tells me she would only be more beautiful if she were sleeping after a thorough fuck.

Sadie murmurs a sweet sound and begins to stir. I remove my finger from her face, but I don't stand. Instead, I stay at her height and watch her so I can be waiting with a smile as her fluttery eyes fully open.

When they do, she shoots her eyes open in surprise that I'm here.

"Hey," I whisper.

She slowly comes to sitting up. "Oh, hey. Sorry, must have fallen asleep."

I sit on the coffee table behind me because I enjoy being at the same eye level with her. "Understandable, I am really late."

"It's okay, really." She yawns then stretches her arms above her head which only pushes her chest out. Christ, those are some perky globes.

"Doing some light reading?" I indicate my head to her book that I put on the coffee table.

Sadie grabs a throw pillow to bring to her stomach. "Yeah, just an interesting book. Hope to put it into practice."

"What is it exactly you plan on doing again?"

She smiles at me. "I won't bore you with the details."

I get up and speak as I walk. "It won't bore me." I head to a high shelf in my living room with whiskey and perfect crystal glasses to accompany the amber-colored liquid I pour.

"Well..." She gets up and heads my direction. "I will organize programs at the library for kids with special needs in terms of learning disorders, ADHD, autism. It'll really help a bunch of kids and help support their parents too."

"That's definitely the first time I've heard that. Normally it's the usual—marketing, doctor, lawyer," I explain as I offer a glass to Sadie.

She indicates no with her head then tilts her chin up. "Usual?"

"I just meant I've never met someone like you and what you do." I drink from my glass, hoping that was a smooth save, because I'm aware she probably has the image that I'm a player in her head. Wouldn't be far off, but not exactly correct either.

"Right. And you've met a lot of women." She tries not to look at me, and I feel like she doesn't enjoy that fact.

"How did you get into that area of expertise anyhow? The education part, not the questioning of my interactions with the opposite sex." I give her a cheeky look.

"I don't know. Thought about teaching, then switched to psychology, realized I could combine both. During college, I volunteered at the local library, and one semester I assisted a special education class at a local school as part of my elective. So, I guess it makes sense how all my interests led to one path."

"Sounds like you made the right choices to find something you enjoy doing."

She shrugs a shoulder.

After a pause, I bring it up again. "Sorry again about being so late. I can't say it won't happen again either."

"It's okay. Everything alright at work?"

I look into my scotch glass. "I don't want to think about it. I'm sure it'll be fine, but my mind is a little fried by now."

For some reason, we have plenty of options of places to sit but we remain a short distance apart, standing with our eyes holding.

"You enjoy what you do?"

"I do. Got into financials after studying economics in college. I worked my way up in analytics and now have my own hedge fund."

The corners of her mouth slant. "That wasn't really an answer. What about it makes it enjoyable?"

It seems she isn't just making conversation; she actually wants to know.

"The rush, the risks, the rewards. You get it all, and it's constantly changing. No day is the same. Are you sure you don't want a drink?" I ask again.

"No, I should probably go. I was one episode away from finishing the latest season of *Peaky Blinders,* but I can save that for another day," she mentions as she heads to the kitchen counter and seems like she's about to gather her stuff.

Taking a decent sip of my drink, I don't hesitate. "Finish the episode. I haven't seen it either. I could use the distraction before checking the overseas markets."

She looks at me with reluctance, but I don't see a hard no coming either. She's as intrigued as I am about staying. The chemistry between us isn't in my imagination.

We have it.

We're just floating around the potential ideas in both of our heads about how to handle it.

"I guess one more episode wouldn't hurt." That delicate smile of hers is going to be the death of me. It's all parts flirty, innocent, and sweet. It may be her standard look, but it feels like it's only meant for me.

My arm goes out to indicate the way, and within a minute, we're both sitting on the couch with the TV on. I'm aware this is becoming a habit, sitting and talking when I return home, but it's refreshing having someone to talk to, and it's a comforting feeling knowing for the summer she will be waiting for me every time I come home from work.

"When do you have time for TV?" She gives me side-eye with a curious look.

Sinking into the sofa and letting my feet find the coffee table, I sigh. "Sometimes on the plane when traveling, rare occasions when I take a break from reading e-mails at night."

"You make it sound like you only ever work, but something tells me you have a lot of fun too."

I laugh to myself. "I try to get out once a week, but you don't have me convinced you're a book worm either."

"Maybe," she answers coyly before focusing on the screen.

But I don't want to focus on the screen, and the fact that her eyes find mine again tells me she doesn't want to look at the screen either.

"By the way, I got box seats for a game next week. Could you meet me there with Mason? We can all watch the game then."

Her eyebrows go up. "I'm joining? Don't you want some alone time with him? It might be good before the twins arrive. Plus, I may have plans."

I give her a closed-mouth grin. "You don't have plans, and I don't think he minds if you're there. You really want to say no to box seats at Wrigley?"

"Not… really. Fine." After a moment, she nudges my shoulder with her hand. "He really looks up to you, you know."

I look forward and think about her words. "I guess so.

I've always been the only guy in his life. He's my nephew, godson, and he doesn't know it, but if something happened to Zoe then he would live with me."

"Are you afraid something is going to happen?"

I contemplate what to say, as nobody has ever asked. It's an instinct to be honest with Sadie, as we have an unapologetic ease of conversation together. "I don't know. She is lying in a hospital as we speak, so it's hard not to think about that."

Sadie caresses my arm and gives me a reassuring look. Her touch is magical and warm. I'm not used to a woman actually caring what I'm saying. "She'll be okay. It's just a precaution now."

"It is."

"Do you want kids one day? I mean, you agreed to be Mason's guardian."

My lips quirk. "No. I think it's different when it's your own child as opposed to your nephew. You?"

Sadie tucks a few loose strands of hair behind her ear. "One day, yeah, I do want kids."

We look at one another and say nothing, completely ignoring the television.

"Are you sure you don't want a drink?" I offer again.

"Maybe a sip?"

Our eyes are locked, and I know a pleased look forms on my mouth. I tilt my glass, holding it up for her. Her lips part. The moment her lips touch the glass, I'm turned on purely by the fact our mouths have touched by way of a glass. She is tasting not only the whiskey but my own mouth. When her eyes peer up to mine as she slowly takes a sip, we both know.

We both know that this is far more sensual than a simple taste.

Her mouth retreats and she licks her lips, and this image

is going to be imprinted in my head and be on repeat later when I'm in the shower.

"I don't think we're going to watch the show. I should go." It comes out softly from her.

I want to say *don't go*.

"Let me check downstairs. It's late, and I don't want you taking a cab."

Pulling up my phone from my pocket, I quickly dial downstairs and never let our gazes break. Quickly I chat with Jimmy at the desk then hang up.

"Sleep here."

Her face looks perplexed, and I quickly clarify. "Jimmy is waiting with poor old Mrs. Smith from the tenth floor for a doctor, and his replacement isn't coming for another hour. I don't feel comfortable getting you a cab this late, and I can't leave Mason to drive you home. Stay here. In the guest room. It's late, and I think you just want to lie down anyhow."

The air feels thick. For me, it's because the idea of this woman sleeping under the same roof as me and not in my bed is quite literally a challenge that I seem to be volunteering myself for.

"I-I guess that makes sense." She doesn't sound unsure; she almost seems like she's enjoying this situation that teases us both.

"I mean, when the twins are born, then I will most likely need you to stay overnight a few times for Mason, so I can go to the hospital." I say it like it's so simple and justifiable.

She quickly adds, "That makes complete sense. Oh, for sure."

We each smile softly at the other that we're on the same page. I swing my feet off the coffee table and stand, offering my hand to pull her up, and her warm delicate hand accepts. I give her a tug and she comes to standing and gives me an appreciative look before letting my hand go.

I make no mistake that her hand fits perfectly in mine. It's duly noted in my brain.

"Let me show you to bed… I mean, *your* bed."

She smirks to herself and her lips curl in. As she follows me down the hall, I stop in front of the door to the guest room.

"I guess this is me," she says.

Scratching the back of my head, I suggest, "Want something to sleep in?"

Her face forms a sexy smile. "It's okay. I don't need to sleep in anything."

That's what I like about Sadie. Unexpectedly she'll say something to purposely taunt me and squeeze my balls—metaphorically.

My tongue glides along my inner cheek from pleasure of all this. "Sounds like an excellent plan, but I can't guarantee Mason doesn't run in here in the morning since he doesn't know you're here." I hold a finger up to her to indicate to wait.

Heading to my room, I return with a t-shirt. I know it will cover all her assets, as she's shorter and tinier than me.

"Thanks." She takes the shirt from my hands.

"Just sleep in, I normally drop Mason off anyway."

"Do you ever sleep in? You barely sleep." She seems to have observed the fact that it's late and I will be awake again in about five hours.

I step closer to her to ensure we are within breathing distance of each other, my fingers reaching and brushing some of her hair behind her ear. "I do sleep in, when there's a good reason to." I can't figure out if my tone is a warning or a simple fact for her to consider.

"Night, Logan," she whispers as her cheek rubs into my hand and fingers.

"Night, Sadie Bay."

Internally, I'm scolding myself for thinking I may need to interrupt her during the night.

8

LOGAN

In the morning, I didn't see Sadie. I really wanted to. I'm beginning to think I would commit murder just to see her walk into the kitchen wearing only my shirt, and I'm curious how angelic she would look in the morning. But I had to get Mason to camp after he asked why Sadie's things were still here and the guest room door closed.

I told the kid the goddamn truth. I was late getting home, and Sadie was tired—I left out the part about her probably enjoying getting eye-fucked by me.

I had too much to tackle at the office to come back and offer her breakfast, but I left her a note on the coffee machine that I hoped she enjoyed Hotel Jax and that the coffee is a special Colombian blend. I'll see her this afternoon when she brings Mason to see Zoe.

Not going to lie, receiving a text mid-morning from her paused my frustration over the Vey deal. Seems she has the ability to calm me, and she doesn't even know it.

SADIE

Hotel Jax gets a 4-star rating. Thanks. See
you at 3!

Quickly I type:

Only 4 stars? Recommendations for
improvements most welcomed.

I watch the dots on my phone frantically bouncing and
stopping.

We can discuss another time.

A little yellow face appears with a smile.

Something tells me she's thinking dirty thoughts like I
am, because in my head, I would only earn five stars if I was
able to have her in my bed and do things to her that would
make her blush for days.

It puts me in a happy mood for the most part of the day,
before debating numbers with one of my analysts, then
heading to the hospital.

I told Sadie to bring Mason to Zoe even if I wasn't there.
They have strict visiting hours at the hospital, and I don't
want to cut Mason's time short. Making my way out of the
elevator, I flash a smile to the nurses by the desk and head
down the hall to my sister's room. I made sure she got only
the best.

Before I even turn into her room, I can hear the
laughter; two women who most likely hit it off from the
get-go. The moment I arrive in the room, I know I'm in
trouble.

Zoe and Sadie are laughing together while Mason is
sitting on the end of the bed eating from the tin of cookies

that he and Sadie seem to have brought. They all look up at me.

"Should I be scared?" I ask with a grin as I bring my sunglasses from on top of my head to hang on my collar against my chest.

My eyes greet Sadie for the first time since last night. Her eyes are bright today, maybe there's even a twinkle I see.

"I was just telling Sadie about the birthing class you attended with me. I was about to share a story from our high-school days—"

I shut that down. "You're clearly feeling cheery today," I comment to my sister.

"I am. I mean, I get to see my favorite son, and he and his lovely nanny brought me cookies with Skittles." Zoe smiles, giving me a look that tells me she has formed a theory in her head. I know her brain; we shared the same cocoon for nine months, and it created superpowers between us.

"Hey, Sadie, you're single, right?" my sister continues.

Sadie looks like she is awkwardly being put on the spot, and she absolutely is. "Uh… yep, I'm single."

My sister gives me an evil glance. "You know, I know someone who would be perfect for you. Logan has a friend, Cole—"

"He is not available." I jump right in there with the lie of the century, because there is no way in hell I am even going to try and entertain this idea.

"Oh, a shame," my sister replies.

Sadie looks between my sister and me before focusing on Zoe. "Well, it was good to meet you in person. I'll get out of your hair and let you guys have some family time." Sadie smiles at my sister. She then touches Mason's shoulder. "I'll wait for you guys downstairs."

"Can we go swimming again?" Mason asks.

"Hmm, maybe not tonight, but next week for sure."

Sadie walks toward the door, and as she passes me, she says, "Meet you downstairs?"

"Yeah, sounds good," I reply.

Not my smoothest of lines, but it works in this situation as I watch her stride out of the room, her body drawing me in more every time.

Refocusing my attention, I look to my sister who has firmly crossed her arms. I wiggle a smile on my face and walk toward the bed.

"She seems really sweet," Zoe notes. "Mason seems to like her too."

"I do," the kid pipes in, completely unaware that his mother and I are entering a standoff of sorts, with her having the upper hand. "She even spent the night last nig—"

A nervous laugh escapes me. "Why don't you go get some crackers from the vending machine," I suggest and urge my nephew off the bed then grab a twenty-dollar bill from my wallet and hand it to him.

The moment he's out of the room, I turn to my sister who gives me a stern look.

"Unbelievable. You're already sleeping with the nanny?!"

I go to sit on the chair by the window. I maintain my cool-as-a-cucumber persona as I lean back with my arms resting on the arms of the chair. "Relax, I am not. She slept in the guest room since I got home really late. What do you mean already?"

"The whole time I looked into nannies, I thought, 'Shit, there will be a twenty-something woman prancing around my brother's penthouse. My brother who most definitely will notice and would have no problem acting on that.'"

"Well, that's not fair. I have done my best to remain a

gentleman. Plus, I told you to find some old nanny whose name is Hilda and who smells bad," I tease.

"But you want to sleep with her?"

"Whoa. You're my sister, and we are not having this convo. Plus, I met her before I knew she was your nanny. That's a coincidence, huh?" I'm being cheeky.

Zoe gives me a disapproving look. "We're going down this route again?" That's a harsh reminder of that *one* time in my history when Zoe and I were at odds.

Yet I push my sleeves up and ignore her. "Now," I begin. "On a scale of one to ten, how much would I be cast in your dungeon if I were to pursue said nanny?" I pretend to look at my watch.

She rubs her giant belly. "Look, I'm not going to tell you what to do. You should be happy. It's because of you that I feel supported. Just… if you and Sadie do something, then it can't go wrong. Otherwise, we are all stuck in a logistical nightmare for the rest of the summer after she receives your token goodbye gift because you got bored, and she's left heartbroken."

My nostrils feel like they're flaring slightly. The people around me really have this image that I'm an ass. *Not cool.*

"Logistical nightmare" she reminds me with firm words. "We can't have that now."

I blow some air out of my mouth. "Don't I know it."

"You are such a cliché. Two seconds here and I saw you looking at her like she's your next meal. Hooking up with the nanny, geez." Zoe now finds this funny.

"Don't worry about it. You have a bigger situation on your hands." My head indicates toward her belly.

"They'll be here soon. You'll come when it's time?"

"Wouldn't miss it for the world. I'm there, delivery, after delivery, whatever you need."

"You're the best big brother in the world." She gives me a loving smile.

There's a pause, and I know I need to ask. "Any news from Steve?" The father of her twins. I've only met him a few times, and he seems decent, but he won't make it back for the birth.

My sister looks somberly at her belly. "We video chatted the other day. He can't exactly tell me where he is right now, but as soon as the girls come, then hopefully he can take leave. I don't know… We're new, and he says he wants to be involved, but what if something happens to hi—" Her mouth quivers.

Quickly, I come to sit on the bed, and my arm goes around her shoulders for a hug. "Hey, it's going to be okay. You have Mom, Dad, me—and Mason seems pretty stoked about his big-brother duties."

"I know."

There's a long moment as we take in the gravity of the situation.

"One lady will be very lucky someday. The things you do to help me, imagine doing that for someone you're in love with. It'll happen to you again. You'll settle down."

"Maybe." It's all I manage to say, and I'm thankful she doesn't bring up why it would be again.

———

"Thanks for sticking around for another hour. Really needed to take that call for work," I tell Sadie as she finishes cooking in the kitchen.

On the way back from the hospital, I was about to have the driver drop her off at her place, but then Jen phoned me to let me know about an emergency call for work that I needed to take. A normal family would let the nanny go at six pm so she can have a normal evening—I coaxed her to stay.

I took the call in my bedroom and changed into jeans and a t-shirt.

"It's not a problem. Plus, tomorrow and the weekend, I'm off." Sadie brings a pan from the stove to the counter and places it on a towel.

We haven't had a minute alone since last night. I don't think we're avoiding one another, just purely logistical that we haven't had time alone.

"Well, your dinner is ready. Mason was reading about a cactus that eats chili yesterday, so ta-da, here is his chili evening." Sadie's hands make a gesture like a magician. "I'm going to head of—"

"No, you are not. Don't be ridiculous." I shake my head at her. She looks slightly surprised. I clarify, "I just mean that we have plenty of food. The least I can do is make sure you're fed before heading home."

She still looks unsure. "Don't you want some alone time with Mason?"

I step closer to her—a respectable distance from one another, but we both get a whiff of each other, and it's almost intoxicating. Sadie puts her hands in her back pockets as we undress one another with our eyes—or at least that's what I'm doing.

"It's just dinner. I'll watch a movie with him after. I'm going to show him *E.T.*"

Sadie's hand flies up and there is a sassy palm in the air telling me to stop. "Bad idea. He'll get nightmares, he's only seven," she reminds me.

I smile at her before going to grab a can of Diet Coke from the fridge. "Nah, he'll be fine. I was his age when I watched it."

"I don't know. Something tells me you may have a guest in your bed."

I freeze in the fridge, taking a moment to enjoy her words. Slowly I close the door to the fridge and face Sadie again with a wicked smile on my face. "A guest in my bed?" My eyebrows raise in amusement.

She nibbles her bottom lip and shakes her head. "What I meant is that most likely Mason will have a nightmare and come to you during the night."

"Oh, disappointing," I reply.

"Anyhow, dinner is getting cold. Mason, food is ready," she calls out and grabs a plate. Mason meets her at the counter, and she helps him dish food onto his plate.

"Is there cheese? I want cheese on my chili," my nephew asks.

Sadie, like the talented child whisperer she is, looks at Mason with feigned shock. "Who doesn't like cheese? Of course we have cheese."

Within minutes, we're all sitting at the dining table.

"You're with Grandma and Grandpa this weekend," I remind Mason.

"Can't I stay here?" His little eyes look at me, and I struggle not to cancel on my parents.

"Sorry, kiddo, I need to work. Next weekend we'll do something, I promise."

"But can't I just stay with Sadie?"

Sadie slows her chewing and isn't quite sure how to answer.

"Sadie has the weekend off, buddy," I explain.

Mason turns to Sadie and pulls her arm. "What do you do on a weekend off?"

I wonder that too, kid.

Sadie comes down to Mason's eye level. "Well, I'll probably go shopping. Meet a friend for a walk at the beach and read."

"Meeting a friend?" I enquire with my inquisitive look.

She's on to me, which is why she gives me a look. "Yes, meeting an old friend from high school who is back for the weekend."

Mason asks to be excused, and I tell him to go get his pajamas on so we can watch a movie, and it means Sadie and I are alone at last.

"Your weekend is missing some excitement," I comment to her as I lean back in my seat.

"How so?" She mimics my way of sitting and tone.

"There are many options, Sadie." My eyes should be warning her that my mind has a few fantasies we could play out.

"Maybe, but I wasn't exactly going to tell your nephew that I plan on drinking a bottle of wine at some point… that's probably *not* one of the options you're thinking."

I smile. "You're a mind reader now?"

"You really never read my resume, did you?"

"Nope. Left it to Zoe."

"Your sister is really sweet. She had a lot of questions about how Mason is doing living here. I said it's only been a few days, but he seems settled and happy." Sadie gets up and begins to collect dishes, and I follow suit. "Are you nervous if you have to stand in for your mom while Sadie is in the delivery room?"

"Yeah, I'm the guy who went to some labor course in case my sister loses her sanity and thinks she needs my help in that process. Just hope my nieces decide to come outside of office hours."

Sadie laughs. "Don't think it works like that. You really

should work less. Maybe you need to rebalance your work/life ratio."

"One day maybe." I shrug as I set a pan back on the turned-off stove. "Why are you so wise for someone your age?"

She throws a towel near the sink. "Because my parents are workaholics—both lawyers. That's not how I want my adult life to be. I mean, look outside, it's summer in the city. People should be enjoying the weather, the sites, the warmth of the evenings mixed with festivals and live music. Not stuck on their phone for a twelve-hour workday."

I like her whimsical view. "Like me, you mean?"

She studies me as she considers what to say. "Nah, you have it in you to be a decent human." Sadie walks by me and pats my shoulder. "I should go."

No, you shouldn't. Stay. Tell me how I'm a decent human. We send my nephew to sleep early. I touch your face, and I plant my lips on yours. Your fingers will play with my buttons as you sit on my lap and tell me you want to hear how we can make your weekend exciting.

"You could stay for the movie," I try my luck.

"Tempting, but another time. I need my own bed tonight. Plus, I need to try and find a printer first thing in the morning." She grabs her bag from the counter.

"Yeah, another time, we have all summer, right?" I walk with her to the front door.

She turns to me, and we stare at one another, as if we're trying to learn how to trace the outline of each other's bodies. "All summer," she repeats, and it's floaty and pure saccharine, before she heads into the hall to the elevator.

"By the way, why do you need a printer?" I ask, slightly baffled.

"I need to print my thesis to send to this publication. Finding a printer isn't easy, to be honest, in this modern age."

"Just come to my office, you can use ours," I offer without hesitation.

"Are you sure?"

"100%." *Hell, I'll even kill a few trees to make this happen.*

"Okay. Well, if you don't mind—"

I interrupt, quite eager. "I don't mind."

Her delicate look and nod are about to make me turn into lava from a volcano—warm, slow, and erupting from the tip.

We aren't even a week in, and I am losing my restraint.

———

THE NEXT DAY IS FRIDAY, and I'm looking out my office window with my hand on my hip. I'm not amused with what I'm hearing.

For the last ten minutes I have been listening about how the key factor that may lose me a potential client is that William Vey is a family man, and he wants to partner with someone who is, well… settled down. He doesn't seem to be a fan of my single lifestyle. Not when a competitor is a family company, complete with a CEO with a wife and two kids.

"So, Vey arrived with his wife for the weekend?" I ask yet again, knowing the answer.

Jen stands hopelessly in the middle of my office. "Yes. They'll be leaving tomorrow at lunchtime."

An awkward silence graces our pause while I think of how to save this, my hand squeezing my jaw.

''Maybe you can bring someone to dinner, so his wife isn't alone while you and Mr. Vey discuss business?" she hesitantly suggests.

My head tilts to the side. Not a crazy idea. "I guess every bit helps."

For the most part, I've kept my romantic trysts separate from my work. Sure, occasionally I would bring someone to a black-tie event or dinner, but for the most part—no. I'm a beast when it comes to business talk, and having someone with me who is no more than a good time is distracting.

Tonight, I need someone who is elegant, smart, and will hang accordingly on my arm. Someone who can play the part and keep me calm.

"Do you know someone?" Jen asks.

I'm about to completely complicate my life to no end, but this is too fun to pass up, and I need her to ensure I close this deal.

"Yeah, I do know someone—Sadie." I can already feel the droll grin forming at the thought of how this all could play out.

9

SADIE

When I arrive at Logan's place of work, his assistant seems to be expecting me. I could swear she's eyeing me up and down, as if I'm under review, but my long summer dress keeps me covered, and I threw on a little jean jacket over my bare shoulders, so I don't think it's my outfit.

"So, you *are* the nanny." She smiles to herself. "I'm Jen, Logan's assistant. Logan is in a meeting but made me promise to take care of you." She stands from behind her desk and is wearing heels and a perfectly tailored green dress. Her glasses seem more fashionable than a necessity.

"Lucky me, I guess." I shrug.

"Trust me, pumpkin, it's going to be your *very* lucky day."

She indicates for me to follow her, and I do, until we're at a little corner in the hallway with a big printer. Nobody really notices me, except for the occasional passerby. It's an open-plan office, with each desk having several screens, I guess for looking at financial data. There are a few private offices with glass walls. It's a modern place, and everyone seems to be happy working here.

"You can just put your USB here and then hit the green button after you pick the sizing on the screen," Jen explains about the printer.

"Perfect. Thank you so much," I reply.

Jen straightens her posture, letting her fingernails tap the wall. She seems to be studying me again. "He'll probably find you soon."

"Oh? I just assumed he's busy." I begin to play with the buttons on the screen of the printer.

"He is very busy, but over the last week he has been doing unusual things, like have me get cupcakes and rearrange his schedule so he can get home at a decent time. And now I know why," she mentions before she walks away with a sly smile.

It only takes a minute before I'm printing. A few minutes later, I'm still only on page fifty of ninety, and I let my eyes wander the place. This is Logan's other sphere where he lives. I wonder if he's bossy or if people are afraid of him. Jen doesn't seem scared of him. I can imagine he is quite different when working. When he's at home with Mason, he's quite casual and laidback, and it makes me soft in my chest when I see how much he cares for the little boy.

Leaning against the wall next to the printer, I also think about what Bed Logan would be like. I bet he has some skills. His hands seem like the perfect size for holding my thighs in place as his tongue runs rampant, and when he plunges into me, his whispers would be crude and make me tingle repeatedly.

Holy moly, I'm making myself warm.

Sadie. I hear my name a few times before I internally knock myself back into the present.

Those blue eyes… he's looking directly at me from not even a foot away. I look at him in that suit, and then turn to the printer, and I realize my papers are done. I'm quickly becoming a frazzled mess.

"Hey, thanks again for letting me use your printer." I grab the papers from the tray and turn my back to Logan so I can curse silently to myself, because in my mind, he was about to make me come.

"No problem. Walk with me to my office? I have a few minutes and need to talk to you about something."

I turn to him, and I'm slightly afraid about what's coming. If it weren't for his smug look, I would feel like a student getting dragged to the principal's office.

"Sure," is all I can muster.

Stacking my papers, I throw my bag over my shoulder and follow Logan. We arrive to his office, and I'm struck by an amazing view of the city. I can't help but walk to the window to look out at the street down below.

"Great view," I note. Turning around, I see he's bringing me a bottle of water and has one for himself. They must have been on his little table of drinks near his sitting area in the office. I take the bottle from him, and he goes to lean against the edge of his desk with ankles and arms crossed and a subtle grin on his face.

"Not complaining about the view today at all," he mutters, and I notice his eyes are on me, not the window. He returns to a normal tone. "Jen helped you okay?"

"Yeah, she was helpful. She seemed to be, well… I don't know… analyzing me. Are you two close?" I have no idea why that escapes my mouth.

"As in she's been my assistant for years and I made sure she had a romantic dinner for two for her birthday a few weeks back?"

My words hit a blockage in my throat; I hate the idea that his words spin in my head.

His grin widens. "Relax. I did get her a romantic dinner for two a few weeks back—for her and her wife." He watches as the dots connect in my head.

Relief floods me, and I roll my eyes to the side to avoid looking at him. Against my better judgment, I step closer to him and let my fingers glide along his dark wood desk fit for a king.

"Everything okay?" I ask, remembering he wanted to speak. "You mentioned we needed to talk."

"Do you have plans tonight? I need your help." He steps in my direction which closes our distance.

I open the bottle of water to keep my hands busy from wanting to touch him, like it's second nature. "Sure. Need me to watch Mason?"

He almost chortles under his breath, as if something is amusing only to him. "Mason is with my parents. I need your help in another way…"

My eyes flick up to meet his, and it feels like he's enjoying spiking my curiosity.

"Okay. What would that be?" I ask before taking a sip of water.

"I need to close this deal at work, and I need you by my side. Can you please join me for dinner as my pretend significant other?"

I nearly spit out the water I'm drinking. "As in pretending to be in a relationship?"

His face is quite calm-looking considering what he just spewed out. "Yeah, something like that. We can work out the logistics on the ride over, as I have to get to another meeting in about two minutes. I can pick you up or you can meet me at my place, whatever you prefer. Dress to impress and use my card—"

"Whoa, you're already shooting off demands and I

haven't even agreed to partake in this." I can't say I'm flabbergasted, because I feel my lips quirk from entertainment.

"Something tells me you really enjoy it like that. Consider this an option for an exciting weekend. Six? Drinks and then dinner. I'll text you details." He grins so confidently as he strides back towards the door to his office.

He is so quick and assured with his words that I have no opportunity to think about my answer. I've already fallen under his magic spell.

"I mean, this is kind of crazy, but fine. I'll meet you at your place."

He turns to me. "Perfect."

The moment he waltzes out of his office, I know I am royally screwed. I don't need to fake anything with that man, but I can't let him know that.

———

Logan hasn't blinked once. His suave look today is making my insides turn to jelly. His hair is slicked back, and he seems to have changed shirts to match his tailor-made suit. His spicy cologne tints the air and acts as a sort of leash, because he will always be present around me tonight and drawing me in. Then those predatory blue eyes gaze at me, as if I'm something special. I'm not complaining with his look.

Not one bit.

I arrived one minute ago, and it seems I have impressed him. He's watching me, as if he is assessing his trophy, and he doesn't seem disappointed.

A black dress with a V-neck in the front and plunging back is always a winner. I kept my make-up simple, except for a little pink lipstick. My hair is down in natural waves, my heels give my legs extra tone, and to be honest, my whole look tonight makes me feel confident.

Clearing my throat, I ask, "Is this okay? It's your thing. I could change into something else. I brought a few options in my bag."

His palm scrubs his jaw. "Perfection. That's what you look like."

My smile forms from his comment, and my cheeks feel warm.

He steps closer to me, and his hand cups my cheek as his forehead touches my own. This interaction between us feels natural, but I'm aware this is crossing an already-blurred line.

"Thank you for doing this. It's my lucky night clearly."

I can only hum a sound as I step back to create space between us. "Shall we go? You said we need to be there by six, right?"

He nods and follows me toward the elevator.

We glance at one another aimlessly until we make it to the car that's waiting for us downstairs. Must be from his work, as Logan normally drives his Aston Martin.

He holds the car door open for me, and I slide into the backseat with him, and soon we are on our way.

"I forgot something. Need to give this to you." His hand dives into the inner pocket of his suit. "Give me your hand," he requests.

I blink a few times at him, before holding my hand out.

He pulls a ring out from a Tiffany's box. I can't speak as he slides it onto my finger. I can't form words because I feel like I've just stepped onto another planet. There is a giant diamond ring on my finger that would pay for half a house. It's shiny, it's blinding, it's every bit as obnoxious as this twist for the evening.

"I should probably have mentioned that we're engaged."

A sly smile appears on his face, because he must know that this is a whole new line of insanity, and he seems to enjoy that he's playing this game with me.

"Wh-what?" I stare at my finger as I place my hand on my lap.

Logan angles his body to watch me, but I can't seem to look away from my hand.

"We need to be convincing. William Vey likes commitment, so I'll give him commitment. I'm soon-to-be husband of the year." His fingers glide along the skin of my bare arm, sending a tremble to parts that I shaved extensively today.

I raise a brow. "Convincing?"

"As in we arrive a few minutes late, which gives them the impression that we are so insatiable that we couldn't resist a quickie in the car. Then during drinks, I'll touch your hand tenderly as you kiss my cheek. Over dinner you will gush about our upcoming nuptials—I'll let your imagination run wild there—just that we're having a small wedding. By dessert, we give them all indications that we want to wrap up the evening so we can go home and practice baby-making, since we plan to have a lot."

I gulp in some air, as my head suddenly has blotches of color spotting around behind my eyes, and I feel dizzy. Something tells me we will be crossing a lot of lines tonight, and while this news was at first slightly shocking, it now just turns me on and sounds all too appealing.

I'm all in.

SADIE

We're walking from the elevator toward the lounge at the Grand. For the last five minutes, from getting out of the car and working our way up in the elevator, we've been going over the basics.

"Okay, so we met here just like we actually met, via mutual friends," I repeat.

"Yep, we just move that timeframe back six months or so," Logan reminds me as his hand finds my lower back, and that tightens a knot in my stomach, of nerves and desire. This could all get confusing.

"Right. Not a week ago," I declare mundanely.

He stops us, and his other hand finds my hip as he angles his body to me, and his mouth hitches up. "It's been a week since we met." He sounds fond of that fact. "Something tells me neither one of us are complaining."

For a moment our charade is put on pause, and it seems we're talking about reality.

"I guess… I'm not."

"Good… neither am I." His look is pure swoon, and my

body reacts. My tongue swirls in my mouth and my internal walls tense.

He pulls my body flush with his, his arms encircling my middle. We fit together so damn perfectly, and then his lips graze my forehead. *Fuck, I'm done for.*

"Showtime," he whispers.

Before I have a chance to respond, we're thrown into the deep end.

"William, good to see you again." Logan steps away from me but keeps his hand firmly on my lower back. "And you must be Miranda," he greets the well-maintained woman in her early forties.

The couple in front of me are older, well dressed, and seem to take care of themselves in terms of health. Miranda's blond hair is perfectly light, and not a smidgeon of her make-up is out of place.

They say hello.

"And where have you kept this one hiding?" William smiles as he takes my hand.

"This is Sadie, my *fiancée*." Logan glances at me, as if he knows that title makes me want to laugh endlessly.

"I had no idea you were engaged," William comments.

Logan pulls me closer by the side before placing a soft peck on my cheek—perfect firm and soft lips.

"Sometimes you keep the best things quiet. We're very private people," he lies.

I know it's my turn to say something. My fingers come to toy with Logan's gray tie. "It's a bit of a touchy topic at his office as we plan on having a very small ceremony up in Door County, Wisconsin, and his office is just too big for the guest list."

Logan looks at me with warm eyes, and his cheeks tighten. It seems he approves of my answer.

"Oh, I went there once as a child," Miranda mentions as we all start to walk to a table for pre-dinner drinks.

During the next half-hour, I stick to speaking with Miranda about her children. They had three of their own before adopting two more. Conversation with her isn't as boring as I anticipated; she is quite involved at her kids' school and does a lot of volunteer work. She takes interest in what I studied, and I notice the way she occasionally glances lovingly at her husband as he and Logan talk numbers, pensions, and stocks that I don't quite understand. During those moments, my own eyes peek over at my fake fiancé at my side, and deep inside me, I know I could get used to this scene for more than just tonight.

My fake fiancé who so easily rests his hand by my bare knee, a touch so simple, yet it gives me a hint of his talents. He has this aura about him when he is deep in business. Logan Jax is absolutely a leader, knowledgeable and sickeningly persuasive. Not only with the charming smile he has, but his accompanying hand gestures, even the way he drinks his scotch.

Occasionally he gives me a wink and I want to roll my eyes in entertainment, but I maintain composure. My hand rests on his shoulder, and I'm too lost in this unexpected situation to use my brain to question all of this more, or maybe even to remind myself that it's pretend.

"Sadie mentioned you're caring for your nephew for a little bit." Miranda smiles.

I squeeze Logan's shoulder as he speaks. "Yes, my sister is on bedrest to deliver twins. He's staying with us, but luckily I have this beauty to help me." He kisses my cheek. It seems I am fictitiously living with him now and we're forgoing the nanny fact.

"That's great. Family is so important," William mentions

before drinking from his scotch glass. "I'm sure you and your young bride will have one of your own one day."

"Yeah, a big family. Twins seem to be a Jax family tradition," I respond before drinking from my gin and tonic.

Logan's eyes, I swear, gleam slightly at me for my efforts.

A few minutes later, we make our way to the dining room for dinner. Just like one week ago, Logan pulls my arm gently to stop me while the others continue on. There's no difference in the way it makes me feel from last week to now. It sends a wave of excitement through me. The only difference now is what he says.

"Best fake fiancée ever."

I look at him, taken aback. "You've had more than one?"

"No. You're the only one."

"What happens if William comes to you in a few months and asks about our wedding?"

His look is brasher than usual. "First off, by then he will have signed, so I don't need to impress him. Secondly, I can ask you to play the part again."

I scoff a laugh. "You're assuming I'll agree, and by the way, maybe I will have met someone by then."

His eyes darken as his hand comes to my face, his thumb drawing a line along my jaw. The whole move will have me succumbing to anything. "Trust me, you've already met someone."

The way he says it almost feels like he's insinuating him, and it makes me smile again, before he takes my hand and I follow him to our table.

Through dinner, we continue the charade, mixing facts with fiction. I wonder why I'm having so much fun, and I'm slightly concerned that it involves deceiving a perfectly nice couple.

"I'm happy to know a little bit more about you, Logan. I

do feel it's important that someone who manages my financials has good character," William explains.

"Ask away, William. You know I can handle the numbers. You're seeing my city, meeting my fiancée, know my sister is about to pop twins. What more do you want to know?" Logan is almost defensive, yet he still plays it cool and leans back in his chair after setting his steak knife down on his plate.

"Any skeletons in your closet?" William gives a serious look.

Logan swirls the red wine in his glass. He sighs. "An ex-wife from ten years ago, a bad investment in a wine company when I was twenty-five—since corrected tenfold—and a speeding ticket from six months ago. Anything else you want to know?" He sounds almost cocky.

My body tenses and maybe he feels it, as he squeezes my hand. I've learned a new fact.

Logan was once married.

I had no idea, and it never came up. Ruby never mentioned it, and there are no signs anywhere. A spark of jealousy flares in me, which is odd, since I have no claim to him. But I don't think I like the idea of him with someone else, even if it's settled history.

It does, however, confirm my theory that Logan really isn't the relationship type.

William barks out a deep laugh. "I appreciate your honesty."

"I don't play games when it comes to my company, William." Logan almost sounds impatient.

The moment is slightly tense, but then I'm relieved when the corners of William's mouth tilt up in an almost smile.

I decide to break the moment. "Miranda, you should try the lemon meringue pie. I tried it last week when someone recommended it to me." I glance at Logan, and it makes his face lighten slightly.

Ten minutes later, pie and coffee are placed in front of us.

"You're going on a boat tour tomorrow? Those are really fun," I tell Miranda.

She smiles then touches my arm. "We are. I asked William to change the flight so I could work in some shopping. Where did you get your dress? I would love something like that. I mean, I know you're younger than me, but I try to keep my fashion trendy."

I laugh. "You can pull it off easily, and I've had this dress for a while. You should check out Water Tower Place. I was there today to check out the sales, but then my fiancé phoned, and I got distracted." I wink at Logan who now has a grin permanently on his face.

"I'll make it up to her, I'm sure." Instead of kissing my cheek, he plants one on my neck below my ear, and it sets a fire between my legs. My skin warms, and his breath teasing my skin feels electric.

"You two are going to have some honeymoon. Where is the destination?" William asks.

"Oh, uhm, Colombia, actually—the Caribbean coast," I say. "I studied a semester in South America but never made it to Colombia, and Logan is eager to make my dreams come true." I interlace our hands on the table for dramatics.

"And the closest I've made it is Panama. Of course, we'll take it easy up in Wisconsin after the nuptials."

"Sounds adventurous," Miranda gushes.

Ten minutes later, we bid them goodbye as a car comes to pick them up and bring them back to their hotel.

The moment their car is in the distance, Logan grabs both of my hands to angle my body to his.

I guess this is where our fake relationship ends. A glimpse

at what a world would look like if he was the type to settle down and I would be the one he wants. Disappointment washes over me, but then pauses when I notice he's staring at me.

He gives me an inviting look. "Let's head back in for a drink, just you and me."

LOGAN

Overlooking the lights from boats floating on Lake Michigan, the warm breeze is perfect. Fresh drinks are quickly brought to us as Sadie and I sit next to one another on the sofa on the outside terrace of the sixteenth floor.

I have no illusions. I didn't need to up the stakes of the game and make her my fake fiancée—a fake girlfriend would have sufficed. But I like to have fun, and it was too easy to pass up, and she was game.

"I should probably give this back to you now." She has a sheepish look as she wiggles her hand sporting my ring on it in the air. It looks good on her.

"You can in the car ride back. I'm slightly concerned that you're a professional at this gig." I take a swig of my drink.

"This was my first go at it, and I don't plan on making this a regular thing." She also takes a sip of her drink, something minty and clean.

"Why did you agree to join me?"

Her lips part, but no words come out. She looks away, and it feels like she's trying to figure out what to say. Her gaze returns to me. "I don't know, but nothing in me was telling me to say no."

My mouth hitches up at her answer.

There's a pause as we look at one another.

But she breaks it. "*Sooo*… can I ask?" She re-angles her body to face me, and her head finds her propped arm on the back of the sofa.

I lean back. "You mean my first marriage?" I knew that was a bombshell that probably got to her.

She nods slowly in response.

"I was young, it was reckless and not meant to be," I answer simply, and it's the truth.

"How long were you married?"

"Two months."

Her eyes go wide, and if she's a normal woman then an alarm bell is probably ringing in her head.

"That's… well, short." She doesn't quite know how to answer, and I hear it in her voice.

"Kate and I were together for a year, decided on a whim to get married, and very quickly realized we both wanted different things in life." I drink a little extra for this sip.

"Do you still talk to her?" She looks at her drink, and I wonder if she's afraid of my answer.

I quickly answer, "Nope."

Sadie doesn't say anything, but then she nudges my arm. "I'm a little concerned you have an engagement ring lying around."

I give her a reassuring smile. "No need to be concerned, I picked it up on the way back from my office."

"Again, a *little* cause for concern." Her voice is slightly squeaky for effect.

"What about you? I know you're single now, but I can't

imagine you've always been that way." Now it's my turn to figure out her history.

She shrugs a shoulder. "I broke up with my ex a few months ago. We were together for a year and half, but it ran its course. I guess you know it wasn't meant to be when you never second-guess your decision to end it. You should think *what if we had worked out*, and I don't."

Couldn't agree more.

"Just dating since then?"

She shakes her head no. "I tried but decided to focus on my move back here to the city."

My eyes must be bugging out, because everything in my body enjoys the fact that she's had a pause and is, in a way, untouched.

"Fact or fiction. You studied abroad in South America?"

A wide smile forms on her face. "Fiction. Your trips to Panama, fact or fiction?"

"Fiction. A wedding in Door County, is that your dream?"

"Maybe a fact. By the look on your face when I said it, I assume you've been?"

"I have. As kids we went several times with my grandpa and uncle to go fishing. Haven't been back in years, but I would love to head up there again." I enjoy thinking of that memory and the possibility of just getting some time away.

She skims my arm with her fingers. "I haven't been back in years either, but I was reading an article the other month about this bed-and-breakfast there that just won an award, and they make special cherry cookies and cinnamon rolls. I guess if it weren't such a long drive from here then you could take Mason."

"It's about a four- to five-hour drive. I could get a private plane."

Sadie lets a chortle escape and nearly spills her drink.

"What's so funny?" I ask, curious.

She debates what to say. "You have a lot of money, but for the most part you live low-key. Sure, you have a nice place, car, and possessions, but you have no problem walking into a supermarket like a normal person. So, when you say things like getting a private plane… I don't know. It doesn't seem like you, the non-work you." She gently pokes my arm. "I mean, I think you would much rather drive the five hours and take in the scenery."

I smile affectionately at her, as she sees the real me more than most. "True. I need to stay close until the twins are born, but later in the summer, we can try and go." A thought comes to me, and I nudge her arm back with mine because I can't resist. "Might need my nanny to come with."

She rolls her head and grins. "As long as I'm not going there to plan my fictitious wedding, but maybe you need guy time with Mason. I think he misses that."

My arm moves to rest on the back of the sofa around her shoulders. "I know. Once this deal closes then I'll have more time for him. Maybe take him to the science museum or Navy Pier. I don't know."

"See, you have it figured out. The science museum is a winner for sure. They went there at his camp and he keeps asking to go again. He wants to see the submarine exhibit." Her hand finds my knee, and I'm not complaining. I like that she's encouraging.

"He seems to share a lot of things with you."

"Mason is only seven, but he observes a lot, and he is so funny and cute." She pulls her phone from her purse and swipes to show me a photo of him yesterday coming out of camp. The little rascal is posing like a pint-sized version of the rapper *Vanilla Ice*. It makes me laugh.

"Christ, I hope he picked that up from my sister's musical tastes. Sure as hell is not mine."

"What are your musical tastes?"

I smile and pull my phone up, swipe, find a playlist, and send it to her. Her phone immediately pings, and in that moment, I can't help noticing what flashes across her screen. She has no chance to stop me as I grab her phone from her hands too fast.

"Off-limits boss? Is that my name in your phone?" The look on my face must be of a man who struck gold.

She blushes into her hand and bites her bottom lip, clearly embarrassed. "It might be."

I adjust my body to move closer to her, making the gap between us evaporate. My hand reaches behind her head to rest on the nape of her neck and to guide her gaze to me.

"So, I'm off-limits?" I give her a coy look.

"Given the dynamics of our situation... yes, you are."

"So, you renamed me on your phone as a reminder?" My face is frozen looking at her, still taken aback by this unexpected entertainment.

"Maybe," she whispers.

"You would only need a reminder if you felt there was an issue." I want to hear the obvious, because it only confirms that she is in fact attracted to me, as I am to her. She tries to look away, but my finger hooks under her chin and guides her head back. "Is there an issue? Are you tempted by me?"

Her beautiful mouth with a fresh coat of gloss from ten minutes ago opens, and I want to destroy her mouth with my own. She licks her lips. "Are *you*?"

"Sadie Bay, you know the answer just as I know your answer." My nose and mouth move to the spot behind her ear that makes her flinch from my breath.

"Logan." Her voice is thick with want. I hear it, and her

breathing picking up confirms that our moment is about to change.

"Let's get the hell out of here, because I'm telling you I am *not* off-limits." My tone is sharp and to the point. I see a glimmer in her eyes as she nods nervously.

I'm aware that I'm crossing a line, but *oh well,* my life is already chaotic. And she arrived for the evening with a look that tells me she isn't afraid and a dress that has been begging me to run my hands wildly over her.

In record time, we make it downstairs and into the back of the car arranged by my assistant. The moment the door closes, she leans back with her head against the headrest, and her eyes land on me.

"This isn't a fake fiancée thing, right?" she states softly with a droll smile.

I have to smirk at her question as the back of my hand strokes her cheek. "This is a you-and-me thing."

Her fingers touch my lips and I want to suck on them, but I need to reassure her, and fuck me, I wonder why I care so much.

"We both want to," I confirm as I move closer to her. My hand rests on her thigh and the other scoops around her neck. The division between the driver and us is up and the windows are dark, which is a good thing, because I'm not going to ignore what I want tonight.

Leaning in, my mouth finds hers and quickly teases her bottom lip to encourage her mouth to open. She welcomes me, and our warm lips firmly press together. I can taste the mix of mint and alcohol on her lips, but I am aware she is perfectly sober. Her soft lips feel like the best possible gift at this point.

Her hands cup my face as her tongue delves into my

mouth. Our tongues are firm as they twist in a slow sensual movement.

Her murmurs are literally the sound of heaven.

We pull away only briefly to check the damage on one another's mouths from our first long, slow kiss. Swollen, red lips and a flame ignited.

Without hesitation, lips fuse together again, melting into one another for a deep kiss, unleashing a need in me to do every little thing that has been in my mind all week.

Our kisses turn fervent, and my hand travels up her body to her ribs, while a match seems to have been lit for her. Sadie moves to straddle me, and I encourage her by gripping her hips to hold her on top of me.

This gorgeous goddess is literally sitting on top of my cock that wants to spring to full attention but is trapped in my pants.

Her dress is hiked up to her waist, allowing her thin pair of panties to be the only barrier between her and my pants. She's breathless as my mouth drags down her neck. I need to discover every inch of her as quickly as possible.

This woman has been my fantasy since I met her. Kissing her is a thousand times better than I imagined.

Her perfume has been acting like a potion all evening, flowery and strong. With my mouth nuzzling her collarbone, I'm thankful her dress is low on coverage in all the right areas. Her hair is all over the place as she presses her center onto my cock, and Christ, she is wet, I can feel it through the thin layer of fabric that I plan on ripping off.

"You feel so good," I mumble into her silky skin before kissing up her neck back to her mouth.

Our mouths merge together as I pull her closer to me. I don't know where to place my hands because I want them all over her. I want to discover every inch of her body.

"Don't stop, please," she pleads.

I smile against the skin of her ear. "No plans to stop," I nearly pant.

My hand glides up her leg, and I nearly burn my hand from her radiating heat. Quickly, I slide my fingers to touch her between her folds. The feeling of her damp satin panties between us is sending me to the edge of a cliff of anticipation. "Fuck, you are so wet."

Her hands manage to get my tie loose, and she's working on the buttons of my dress shirt as her mouth follows on the journey down. Meanwhile, I crook a finger under the fabric to feel her warm and drenched slit, and I want that sheathed around my cock.

She gasps when my finger strokes along her little pearl, and her glance is seductive as her hands slide up and down my torso between loose buttons.

"That feels *so* good," she moans as I work her pussy with purpose.

I know I'm doing well when her mouth breathes onto my neck and she holds onto the back of the seat to brace herself. Her body moves against the friction of my finger, subsequently rubbing up and down my cock.

"I want your big hard cock inside me," she moans.

"Ah, so you do have a dirty mouth," I tease her and absolutely love it.

She flashes me a fun look before she grabs my other hand and coaxes me to mold it against her breast. Without hesitation, I squeeze that beautiful globe before moving the fabric harshly to the side. I pull down her strapless bra enough so her beautiful taut nipple springs free and meets my mouth.

I lick, I swirl, I suck—and I quickly learn that she likes that a lot.

Her throaty moans are a song of encouragement as

Sadie's hands find my belt and she gets to work on unbuckling.

"Logan." Hers is the only voice I want to say my name in this situation. "Please." Her hand cradling my cock through my briefs feels like an indication that she really wants me inside her.

I fucking want to plunge into her with no delay…

But why does my chest have an unfamiliar sensation?

Sadie is different, I can't explain why. I don't have the usual urge to make it quick and efficient then run. With Sadie, I want time to digest the enjoyment of screwing her brains out. I've never had this wish the way I do with her. I've never felt this uncontrollable need to have someone.

With reluctance, I bring her hands away. Interlacing our fingers, I pull my mouth away slightly to slow us down. I smile at my ability to stop this and at the fact her mouth is a swollen mess.

"Sadie, beautiful. I'm not going to fuck you here."

"No?" Her look is disappointed.

I kiss the knuckles of her hand in mine. "No. I want to take my time with you, get you completely naked. I sure as hell don't want Oscar to hear the way I plan on making you scream." I indicate my head to the front of the car.

She smiles at my humor as I kiss her hand again. That shiny ring flashing at me is a reminder that this woman is possibly something special. Because really? Who agrees to play along as a fake fiancée and seem completely normal-minded?

Sadie hops off my lap, and we both quickly try to straighten our clothes, as we have to manage a respectable elevator ride up to my place.

I lean over and kiss her gently on the lips. They're my lips for tonight, tomorrow, and as long as we can go before it gets complicated.

And this probably *will* get complicated. She's the type of woman looking for a future with someone, a long future. I push that thought to the side. Tonight she's mine.

We arrive at my building, and I take her hand as we make our way through the lobby to the elevator. In the ride up, I gently kiss her forehead, then her cheek, then her lips as I keep her trapped between the wall and me with our bodies pressed.

Damn, she molds perfectly to my body.

"So, what will my title in your phone be after tonight?" I ask softly with a grin.

"Hmm." She pretends to contemplate. "Maybe… the big charmer."

My eyes widen, impressed, as I like that compliment. "How so?"

Sadie looks up at me, her arms still entwined behind my neck. Her humorous look spreads across her face. "Because even though all week I told myself this is a bad idea, your charm can't be denied. I give up. So, yes, you charmed your way into comprehensively fucking the nanny."

12

SADIE

We spill into Logan's place, and immediately I'm tugging his suit jacket off. He lifts me up and my legs wrap around his waist, and I rest my hands on his shoulders. I feel like I'm about to combust. I need his mouth like air, and I would rather sacrifice air if it means I can have my mouth on his without needing to break contact.

He moans, I moan. We're making noises as our bodies entangle.

Let loose—that's exactly what I can do with Logan. I'm doing it now, and I'm heading down a rollercoaster with no way to stop. I'm too addicted to his touch already.

I couldn't even say how we make it down the hall, as I'm too busy pressing my body to his. I love the feeling of his hard length against me. His foot kicks his bedroom door open, and within seconds, he has me planted on his bed. The lights from the city flooding in through the floor-to-ceiling windows give us enough light to see what's happening, while I'm aware of the feeling between my legs of how much I want him.

I move back on the bed and prop myself up on my elbows while I watch him uncuff his shirt.

"I want to watch you undress," he states. It should come out as a request, but it's a demand.

It turns me on, the idea that he will lead us. He'll take me the way he wants. It feels like this is something unique to anything I've done before. It's what I've been searching for. He's skilled, he's experienced, and he's a man who is eyeing me with desire and lust.

Obeying, I come to my knees in the middle of the bed. He's taking his shirt off as his eyes remain fixated on me. My fingers find the zipper on the back of my dress, and the sound of the zipper coming undone fills the air, tooth by tooth. Quickly, I pull the material up and over my head, leaving me in black panties and a strapless bra.

The corners of his mouth tug into a smile as his hands unbuckle his belt. "Keep going," he encourages.

I bite my lip as I unclasp my bra then purposely and slowly hang it in the air by my finger, raising a brow at him before dropping the material to the side. My nipples are already hard and ready for him, tingling from arousal. Deciding I want him to do the honors of removing my panties, I lie back on the bed with my head landing on the pillow. I set one arm above me and the other rests on my belly.

"I want you to finish the job," I rasp, admiring the view of Logan Jax completely naked in front of me. He is the image of perfect physique. His manhood is big, thick, and smooth— very erect too. The thought of what he plans to do to me makes my thighs open, and my bottom lip is getting attacked by my teeth.

The bed dips as he comes to all fours on the mattress and

hovers over me, kissing my mouth. "You are so hot." It comes out tender and slow.

But it's only for a few seconds, because in a swift movement, he quickly slides my panties down and pulls me to the edge of the bed. He brings my legs up, and my feet rest on his shoulders as he unbuckles the clasp of my high heels around my ankles, kissing my inner ankle, and it makes me giggle slightly.

He releases my feet from his shoulders, and he parts my legs open, now resting on the bed. He kisses my inner knee before skimming up my thigh, his hand on my other thigh, mirroring the movement.

My clit is pulsing for him, my inner walls are clenching. I need him.

It's only temporary relief when his tongue licks up my sex. When he sucks on my bead, I gasp from the pleasure, and I could come already.

My fingers twist his hair as I watch his head moving between my legs. His tongue is a magical instrument with moves I've never even felt before.

"So good, Logan. So, ooh…"

I'm not silent, and the way his eyes peer up at me tells me he approves.

When his tongue delves inside of me, my hips buck then tilt up. I want desperately to come on his face, and that internal confession is an awakening. I'm never this honest or free during sex.

Maybe it's because his presence oozes assurances and confidence. He must be experienced, and I trust him to get us there. I trust him in a lot of things, actually. This man stirs something inside of me, but right now, I can't dive deeper into that thought, because he's causing me to feel as though I'm molten, his tongue back at my clit, while a finger dives inside me. All of these sensations cause my own hands to find my breasts to palm.

"Sadie, your pussy tastes better than I imagined," he mentions before returning to my clit.

"*Well*, your tongue is better than I imagined," I barely manage to speak as my body curves from enjoyment. My thighs move wider out of impulse, and I move against his tongue. I'm almost there.

"Oh, God, oh."

I'm convulsing on his tongue, my body shaking as I come. His tongue and finger lighten their strokes as he helps me come down in my freefall, but he's not stopping.

He doesn't stop until I'm sated, and then his mouth places soft kisses up my stomach to my breasts before meeting my mouth at last. My taste hits my lips, making me give a throaty groan. The sound gets swallowed by his greedy mouth that seems to want to ensure I get a taste.

I wrap my legs around his waist and pull him to me, making his cock rub against my clit. His hand holds my neck and jaw in place against the pillow, his breath showering my ear with humidity.

I hum and tremble, and we aren't even done yet, causing my breath to pick up again just from that thought.

"Are you okay?" he asks tenderly with our eyes meeting.

I nod against the gentle force of his hand keeping my head in place.

His thumb rubs my bottom lip. "Good, because I need to feel you coming on my cock." He reaches over to his night-stand and grabs a foil package.

Coming to my knees, I meet him in the middle of the bed. "I want to touch you first, let me," I request.

He smirks approval as my hand reaches down to grip his hard length. My inside walls pulse again with a needy ache for him. Stroking him, I'm flooded with the idea that he will be inside me, and I want it desperately.

"I need you in me. You want that, don't you?" I look into his eyes as my hand works his cock.

With his hand framing my jaw and neck, he contrasts his touch with gentle kisses around my face. "I do, but Sadie, this round I need to go deep and hard. Your pussy has been making me go insane all week," he warns me.

It just makes a new wave of arousal spill out of me.

"I can't wait. Have me whatever way you want."

He kisses me hard and quick on the mouth before opening the condom. "Be careful what you say around me."

Watching him slip the condom over his impressive cock is all parts anticipation and slight fear about whether I can handle him—not just physically either. I like him, I admire him, and even if he will never be mine, I think he could be something special.

Lying back, I let my thighs spread open as the cool air hits my pink flesh, and my nipples grow harder. His heat is welcome when he comes to cage me under him. Our eyes agree to go further.

When his tip finds my entrance, I know he will take care of me in this situation. My juices coat his tip as his hand comes back to my face.

He enters me slowly, and it's a stretch that makes me whimper.

"Sadie, tell me what you need," he urges, and the light from the windows highlights the concern on his face.

"Just… slow at first."

He listens and goes in an inch then retreats back, then goes deeper and back. The moment I feel the discomfort settle, my hands find his ass to urge him to go deeper.

"Take me," I gasp with our eyes locked.

"That's what I plan to do," he warns me as he picks up the pace.

Deep, long pumps hit me all the way in and find that internal button that not many find.

"You know how good you feel?" he asks before kissing me again.

"I don't know. I'm too focused on your big cock doing amazing things to me."

He appreciates my witty comment, shown by the fact he smiles against my shoulder before kissing my skin.

His hand scoops under my knee then he brings it over his elbow, opening me wider. The sensations inside me multiply as his rhythm increases.

I moan, he groans, our breathing grows heavy.

He manages to turn my body by moving my knee until I am lying on my stomach. His mouth trails kisses down my back as his hand brushes my hair to the side. The feeling of his length pushing in and out of me and hitting whole new nerve endings overtakes my body.

"You like it like this?" he breathes near my ear.

"Mmhmm, just like that." My hands claw the duvet as everything grows intense.

My pussy clenches around him, wanting to add extra pull for his pleasure.

"Sadie, I'm getting there."

His finger moves between my body and the mattress to rub me, to help me fall with him. The moment he strokes me, I am right where he wants me.

"Me too."

The next minute is a blur of pure ecstasy as our sweaty bodies slap against one another and our grunts and moans fill not only the room but the entire penthouse.

"Logan," I scream as he comes, jerking slightly inside of me as I shudder from my own orgasm.

"Fuck, Sadie." He collapses on top of my body, but he carefully places his weight on his arms, holding me tightly against him.

We lie there, satisfied, in an embrace as both of our breathing transitions from harsh to steady.

It's only then I realize, with our fingers interlaced against the bed, that the shiny ring is still on my finger. A slight letdown hits me that part of the night will only ever be pretend. Then a spark hits my chest when our eyes gaze into one another's and his thumb strokes the back of my hand and his fingers tighten our hold. Logan places kisses on my back, not once but twice, before nuzzling his nose into my neck, then our mouths fuse for a deep and long kiss.

"Be right back," he whispers.

I don't even move. I can't. I'm completely sated and overcome from the most amazing orgasm of my life.

I hear Logan step out of his bathroom, and he crawls on all fours across the bed. His teeth tease the cheek of my ass before dragging up my back. He lands back into the position he was before he went to take care of the condom. Spooning me from behind, he links our hands and kisses the back of my neck.

His soft kisses make me feel delicate. I hope this need to hold me is different from his past conquests. I want to be unique to anybody else he has been with.

Something special.

Why? I'm not sure. He's new to me, but there is a pull between us that gives me an unwavering feeling that I can't resist.

"You okay?" he asks softly, warmly.

"Mmm." I roll to my back and my hand touches his face,

my thumb rubbing his cheek. "Very okay."

His smirk forms before he kisses me again then moves to lie on his back. His arm encourages me to lie against his chest. Of course, I do. I'm going to soak in whatever tonight is for as long as I can.

There's a long silence as we lie there in complete post-sex bliss and lust.

"I guess tomorrow I can finally give you a five-star review for Hotel Jax," I tease, and he responds by squeezing my arms to him.

"Ah, so our minds were aligned. You needed to be in my bed to earn me a five-star review."

I can't help but giggle. "Exactly."

My eyes see that ring again on my finger, and this time I do something about it. I slide the ring off my finger, holding it up to Logan. "This is yours."

He smiles to himself. "Oh yeah. Nearly forgot about how tonight started." Taking the ring, he sets it on the side table.

But that ring is a reminder of a situation that we most definitely landed ourselves in.

"Hate to ask but—"

"Shh." He discourages me from talking as he kisses my forehead. "We will talk about it tomorrow after I fuck you before breakfast."

Not a horrible idea.

All I can do is sigh as we shuffle under the covers.

"Funny, now you aren't offering me a shirt like the other night," I remark.

"Because now, Sadie, you are in *my* bed. You never need to wear a scrap of clothing when you're in my bed. It's useless. I'll just tear it off." He is so serious when he says it, yet I like the playfulness of the context.

I can only hope that means this isn't a one-time thing.

13

LOGAN

Sadie mumbles into my neck as I plunge into her, the sun seeping through the windows. It's better than I could have envisioned.

It's been a long time since a woman slept in my bed. That was never part of the arrangement with past choices as of late, but it feels right to have Sadie here.

Waking to find her peacefully sleeping in my arms was an image that should have been photographed then placed in a museum. She is beyond beautiful. I can't say innocent, as last night showed me that she most certainly has a dirty mouth, and every part of me likes it.

The moment I woke, I admired her for a minute or two. She followed with waking up, like an animal awakening from hibernation. I kissed her on the mouth, but at the same time, my hand roamed between her legs, and like a good girl, she woke up ready for me.

And five minutes later, I'm taking her slowly. Our eyes dance with one another, and there are soft smiles on our faces.

"You feel so good inside me," she whispers.

I'm on top of her, and I'm cherishing every inch of her body that my lips can reach. I picked up last night that, even though she is all in on the physical part, it's intense for her. She fit snugly around my cock, and the way she responded to my movements showed me that this is not a normal occurrence for her.

I love that. Her body is, in a way, treasured. I'm the guy that gets to bring her to bliss, and I want to make it good for her.

I'm not completely out of my mind. I know there is a conversation coming after our second—okay, maybe our upcoming *third*—round this morning.

But right now, I want to be in this moment. For the first time in years, it feels like not only am I connecting on a physical level with someone, but a mental level.

Our eyes pierce one another, and it only intensifies good old-fashioned morning sex. The best kind of sex for weekends.

"Come for me, baby," I plead with her.

"I will, but please fuck me until *you* come. Don't stop until you come." There is a hint of begging in her voice that turns me on.

"Where have you been all my life?" I tell her with a grin, and while it could be taken lightheartedly, it's the damn truth. We are so compatible in bed, it's pure orgasmic bliss.

We get there. We hit our edge, and we fall together with our mouths soaking in one another's moans.

After a few minutes, I let her rest while I go to the bathroom. When I emerge, I see she's sitting up in bed with the sheet wrapped around her and her hair a perfect mess.

She nervously bites her lip. "So… good morning."

I smile as I grab some clothes from the drawer. "Did we skip that formality this morning?"

"Seems so."

"Let me have breakfast delivered," I say as I throw a shirt on over my body. "The coffee should already be made, it's on a timer."

I come to the bed to kiss her even though I have no clue what I'm doing. I have no answers at this moment in time for what this is.

"So, last night. This morning—"

I cut in, "After breakfast."

She smiles at my suggestion. "We should probably talk. This is kind of complicated considering—"

My phone interrupts us and vibrates on my dresser. It's Saturday morning, but this isn't the first call I've had at this time. "Should probably take that before we dive into conversation," I note.

Quickly, I grab my phone and answer.

The moment I hear the person on the other end, my heart panics. "Yeah, that's me… What?!... Yeah, I'll be there in half an hour." I hang up, and quickly my hands find my hair as I consider what I need to do.

Sadie looks at me concerned. "Everything okay?"

"No. Zoe went into labor, and it's still too early."

———

AFTER GETTING THE CALL, Sadie quickly went home to change since her dress from last night or her wearing my shirt were not good options for meeting me at the hospital. She'll take Mason back to my place, since I know my parents, and they won't want to leave my sister—understandable. How I managed to make it to the hospital so fast, I do not know. I'm probably going to add another speeding ticket to my record, but it's a necessity today.

It all happened so fast. Zoe started having contractions, and there was too much blood, so the doctors felt the best option was a C-section to ensure the twins have the safest arrival at thirty-four weeks. It also meant only one person could be with Zoe for the birth, which was our mom. They were already in the operating room when I arrived. After waiting for what felt like an eternity, I was allowed into her recovery room.

Walking into my sister's hospital room, I slow my pace as I approach her bed. She looks exhausted and groggy.

"Hey, Zo, don't be annoying and speak. You need to rest," I remind her as I grab a chair next to the bed.

"I'm not allowed to see the girls yet. I only got to see them quickly before they rushed them off."

I stroke her hair. "I know. They're in the NICU; Mom and Dad are checking on them. I hear they'll get the VIP treatment. The blankets are high thread count and room service stops by several times a day." I do my best to make her smile.

She just cries. "You'll check on them?"

"Of course, Uncle Logan is here."

"And Mason?"

"Sadie took him back to my place. He won't be allowed to see the twins for a while since they're in NICU and no kids allowed. Don't worry, I told Sadie to go wild with my credit card at the toy store. Mason is fine," I assure her.

"You didn't get to see the birth." She cries harder.

I adjust her blanket as I look at the beeping screens. "It's okay. Something tells me I would have fainted anyways. Now sleep." I decide to leave out the fact that I was never actually thrilled with her idea that I should be around for that fiesta.

"If something happens to me, you'll take care of Mason, Daisy, and Lily?"

A soft smile forms on my mouth. "You are going to be

fine. *Huh…* cute names. Guess you have a garden theme happening."

"It's cute…" It trails off as she falls asleep.

I move in the chair and let an exhausted breath go. Sitting there for a few minutes, I think about being here in this situation, and for the first time ever in my life, I wonder what it would be like if the situation were different—if I would be sitting here waiting to meet my own child. It's not like that's a crazy thought, I've just never thought about kids, and I can't figure out for the life of me why it suddenly crosses my mind.

———

It's midafternoon when I get home. The nurses didn't want Zoe to have any more visitors for the day, so it ended up being a short visit. Looking out my living room window, I admire the view of the city. Even on a cloudy day, it's a relaxing thought that my home is quiet while there's a busy world below. A great thought… until the front door opens and Mason comes running in, Sadie in tow with shopping bags.

"Hey, kiddo," I greet my nephew who runs to the kitchen.

"Hey, Uncle Logan, we went to the toy store." Mason stretches and reaches up to the fruit bowl for a banana.

Watching Sadie placing bags down on the dining table, my lips tug. Our morning was interrupted by the call then flipped upside down by a complete change of plans. We didn't get to have our conversation.

I walk to the table to help Sadie and offer her a faint smile. She isn't ignoring me, but she struggles to look me in the eyes.

"He got a new helicopter and some books," Sadie begins to ramble, turning her attention to Mason. "We got gifts for your sisters too, right, Mase?"

Mason comes to join us. "Uh huh, little clothes and books to read to them."

I pick Mason up under my arm like a football then set him down and crouch down to him. "So listen, Mason, we should talk about Daisy and Lily."

"I can see them tomorrow?" He looks hopeful.

I look at Sadie then back at Mason. "No, buddy. They aren't allowed many visitors, so you'll have to wait until they're stronger. Big brothers your age are just too much excitement for them right now."

"Oh." He frowns.

I bite my lip, unsure of where to take this.

Sadie touches Mason's shoulder. "*But* they would love to receive pictures from you that you draw, and I'm sure your uncle will read them the books you picked out."

"And my mom?"

"She's resting," I tell him. "You'll be able to see her in a few days."

"Oh. Does this mean we're going shopping again to get her a gift?"

Sadie laughs at his comment. "Don't you want to get something nice for her?"

"Yes, but I only like toy stores."

I have to laugh at my nephew still trying his luck.

"How about flowers? You can pick those out, right? We can also make your mom's favorite snacks to take to her," Sadie suggests.

I'm relieved she's here; she's making this easier for me.

"Okay," Mason answers before running off to turn the TV on.

Sadie and I look at one another… a little unsure. I really could use her arms around me right about now, but I'm not sure what the protocol is in these situations.

I indicate my head down the hall and for her to follow me. We go to my room and close the door behind us.

The moment the door closes, I grab her arm and wind her to me, so she lands against my chest. My mouth leans down to try and grab a kiss, but her head tilts away. Instead, she places her palms against my chest and guides me back to sitting on my bed. Stepping between my knees, she looks down at me as her fingers reach for the hair at the back of my neck.

"You okay?" she asks. "It's been a crazy twenty-four hours for you."

"Yeah." I exhale and rest my head against her stomach as my hands rest on her obliques, her fingers running through my hair. "We didn't get the morning I planned."

Her finger comes under my chin to tilt my face up. "You have a lot going on, Logan. We don't need to talk about it. We had a good night, and that's all it needs to—"

I pull her to my lap in a jerk. "I need you in my bed. That's what I need."

Her fingers touch the weekend stubble on my face. "Your nephew is here, and I don't think he needs more confusion. Your sister certainty doesn't need the added stress if she found out."

She has fair points.

"I need to be de-stressed, and you have a method that helps."

She pinches my arm. "Logan, I think given that a lot is going on, and we see each other daily, that maybe we shouldn't sleep together. It's the safest option for everyone."

While this should disappoint me, I'm not convinced that she wants what she's saying.

"What about not sleeping together and fucking like crazy when Mason *isn't* around? Because we have a window of opportunity between 9am and 2pm on weekdays."

Sadie laughs but then turns silent.

Letting her hand drop from my face, she looks serious. "I think you know what I mean."

I nip at her shirt with my teeth, and I mumble, "I do, but I'm not sure I agree." Retreating my head back, our eyes hold.

"I just… don't want to make your life more complicated, and I'm not sure I want a complication either."

"How about this." My fingers toy with the edges of her shirt. "I'll humor you with your method, I'll honor it. But if I charm you, then you in my bed is up for re-negotiation?"

No way is she going to get away that easily, and either way, we will be seeing one another for the weeks to come.

She smiles as she steps away and heads out of my room. "No comment."

I grab her wrist before she can open my bedroom door. "Hey, Sadie."

"Yeah."

"You don't regret last night, right? I mean, we had a good time." The vulnerability in my voice even surprises me—this isn't my style.

She glances away before looking at me. "I had a great time. That's the problem."

I want to evaluate her sentence more, but I know we have a child in the other room.

"I'm happy you're here. I don't think I could handle all of this by myself," I admit honestly.

She gives me that soft nod. I know that something shifted between us in the last twenty-four hours. Unintentionally, we've been thrown together, and something tells me we aren't nearly done yet.

"Whoa, you have a just-fucked glow." Emily grins at me as she lands herself on a high-top chair at a bar in Lincoln Park. Emily places her purse on the bar top. I'm so thankful that she's in town visiting her parents at exactly the time I need her.

It's only eight pm, but the crowd is just right. Not too busy, not too quiet. You can still hear the indie playlist they have playing in the background. The brick walls and artsy glasses lands this place on many blog lists.

I've already been nursing my vodka cranberry for the last ten minutes while I waited for Emily to arrive.

She touches my arm to grab my attention. "Am I right?"

I try not to smile. "I mean, I am a little sore."

And it was completely worth it.

"You and Logan?" Her eyes bulge out from interest.

I nod yes.

"You didn't even last a week."

"It was exactly a week, thank you very much." I should be proud of that fact at least.

"How did it happen? I thought you were off yesterday."

Emily thanks the man behind the bar for her drink, a martini. She takes a sip and waits for my response.

"So, this is where I might look like the insane one of us two. I was with Logan last night for some work dinner he had… as his fiancée."

Emily spits out her drink and her jaw drops.

I hold a hand up. "*Fake* fiancée," I clarify.

"And sleeping with him was part of the show?" Her voice squeaks, and she's trying to regain her composure.

"No. That we decided to do after." I indicate to the barman for a second round.

Emily smiles at me. "Okay. So, what now?"

I break down with a deep sigh. "Well, our morning wake-up was interrupted by an emergency. His sister had her twins early and they're all in the hospital. Logan has a lot going on; I don't need to add more to his plate. He wouldn't have time for me anyhow."

"Sounds like you're putting up a wall, so you don't get hurt. Does that have anything to do with the fact you're on the search for your future husband?"

I roll my eyes. "I'm not looking for my future husband."

Emily scoffs. "Sadie, since sixth grade you started a policy of wanting to find Mr. Right and not wanting to waste time on anyone else. It's why you broke up with your ex. The moment you realized he wasn't husband material, you put on the brakes. Let me guess, your player of a boss isn't husband material but great in the sack?"

My jaw drops low, and my eyes bug out from her honesty, and my throat feels dry from the fact that some of her words are correct. "I-I don't think it's that," I lie, but then continue. "I just feel like Logan is… different. Danger-ously different." Internally, I smile at that thought. I want whatever he's willing to give, even if it's only a few weeks of fun. This isn't me—well, it's never been my style until now, it seems.

"What does he want?"

I bite my lip and twirl some hair around my finger. "Another round. That's the whole problem. It's tempting, but I'm not sure I could keep my feelings out of it. I see him almost daily; I can't escape him. Unintentionally, I'm getting to know him… really well."

"Hmm, sounds like maybe there's something more than attraction brewing?"

I laugh. "Maybe, but where would it go? I mean, it's not like he's looking for long-term."

"So, if he showed up at your door and said he wanted more than a good *ah oh ooh,* then you would consider?"

I think about that. "I mean… I wouldn't slam the door." I play with the thin straw in my drink. "But I've only known him a week. I didn't even know he was once married until last night."

Emily doesn't say anything, but instead stares at me, studying me.

"He is a little older, an ex-wife isn't a big deal. A lot of people have one," Emily jokes and nudges me in the arm.

"That's not even an issue. It's more that I'm an idiot. I just couldn't resist, and even though I knew this would add a slew of complications, I couldn't stop."

"You're not an idiot. You are allowed to have no-strings-attached sex."

"With my boss?"

Emily brings her shoulders to her ear. "I mean, technically that's a coincidence. You met by chance before."

"I think the best policy is to keep everything platonic, and then maybe when Mason is living back with his mom, then well…"

"Ooh, you really want to bang him again. Was it that good?"

I fan myself at the replay in my head. "He is *so* good. It was… I don't know, it felt like we were both crossing lines we'd never crossed before with anyone. I know that's silly, or maybe it's all in my head."

"Maybe you both just have a connection. I mean, you have good conversation with him. Why don't you just enjoy being around him, whether that's platonic or not?"

"Yeah, maybe I will," I reply softly. "Hey, are you sure you don't want to crash at my brother's place tonight?"

Emily's face tightens slightly at the mention of my brother. They're sort of one another's bane of existence, I sometimes sense. They avoid one another and have done for a few years now, but I'm clueless as to why. I mean, one could guess, but I think if they'd ever hooked up, then one of them would have let it slip by now.

"Wes is still away?" she double-checks with me.

"Yeah, hasn't been back to Chicago in weeks."

Emily looks away slightly and taps the bar. "Sure."

I smile, satisfied. "Good. That means we can have another round, which I greatly need."

———

ON SUNDAY, I only texted Logan to check if everything was okay with his sister and the twins, to which he responded they were all doing okay considering. I was impressed he kept his texts innocent.

Monday, I pick Mason up from camp and follow our routine. We head to the hospital so he could see his sisters through the glass window at the NICU, and as soon as we reach the window, my ovaries pop.

I'm frozen at the scene in front of me.

"Look, Sadie, Uncle Logan is with my sisters." Mason pulls my arm.

"Yeah, uhm," I gulp. "I see."

This is not the scene I need right now. I'm not unaffected.

Logan doesn't notice that I'm gaping at him through the window, as he's too busy. He's wearing a hospital gown and is holding a tiny bundle in a pink blanket and sitting in a rocking chair. Is he cooing at the baby? Surely, he doesn't have that superpower too.

One of the nurses says something to Logan, and he looks up at us. He smiles that handsome smirk before focusing on the baby again. I'm not even sure if I'm still on planet earth.

This isn't a fair start to my platonic-Logan week. Family-Logan, complete with a baby, has my reproductive system jumping, and my throat feels a little tight from the emotional sweetness of the scene.

"Where's my other sister?"

I step behind Mason and investigate the room to read the name labels. Finding Daisy's name, I point for Mason, and Mason studies the little baby in awe.

This whole scene warms me inside, and I smile. The next five minutes are a daze as we watch Logan hold the baby then place Lily back in her bed with the nurse's help. Two minutes later, Logan comes into the hallway.

"When can I hold the babies?" Mason jumps and asks.

"Not yet. They need to grow a bit more. Let's go see your mom, she was sleeping before," he suggests and places a hand on Mason's back.

Our eyes meet, and it's something unique. Changed. Soft. Special.

We all make our way to Zoe's room, and she's awake when we arrive. I hand Mason the bag of gifts for his mother and stay in the hallway while Logan gets Mason settled. It doesn't take long before Logan returns to the hallway and closes the door behind him.

He leans against the wall, and I follow suit at a spot next to him. Looking to my side, our eyes meet.

"Zoe wanted some alone time with him," he explains.

"Makes sense."

"She was able to speak to Steve via video, and he was pretty emotional. I think they'll be alright." He looks at the floor as he crosses his arms.

I squeeze his arm. "Sounds promising, and the babies look okay."

He almost glows. "They are cute ones. Lily is stronger, and I haven't been allowed to hold Daisy yet. They'll all be here a while longer."

"You never told me about your baby-whispering talent." I let the words float out of my mouth.

He glances at me. "Wouldn't say that. I was just giving her a lecture to stay the hell away from boys," he jokes.

"Wise advice." I take a moment to observe him and notice he's a bit more somber than normal. Touching his shoulder, I ask. "Are you worried?"

Logan debates what to say. "A little. They say you feel when your twin is in pain. I don't really believe that, but yeah, it isn't great to see your twin sister in an emotional hole, plus with two tiny babies born early."

In that moment, I realize he needs someone to listen, and already against my plans, I interlace his fingers with my own. He looks down at our hands together and the corners of his mouth twist. It just feels right.

"You are a good brother, Logan Jax." And again, because it feels right, I kiss his cheek.

We stare at one another. A friend, that's what he needs

now, and even though I can tell he has other ideas behind his ocean-blue eyes, he knows that in this moment a friend is what he needs.

————

THE NEXT DAY, Mason and I are sitting at a booth in the busy restaurant. I cut a piece of deep-dish pizza for him.

"This is my favorite." Mason grabs his fork.

"Mine too," I tell him, sliding the plate over.

"Enough for me, I hope?" Logan arrives with his smooth grin plastered on his face. Of course, Mason's face lights up.

"If you're in the market for BBQ chicken with pineapple, onions, and mushrooms, then yes," I reply as Logan slides into the other side of the booth. "He was hungry, so I went ahead and ordered for him."

"Sounds good. Did you order us a bottle of wine?" Logan looks at me with smoldering eyes, only magnified by the fact he is still in his suit from work, and I want to playfully slap him for already heading us down this route for the evening.

I proudly take a sip of my iced tea. "No, I did not. Didn't think I should be drinking while watching your precious nephew."

"Well, you're off nanny duty now, so feel free to have a drink with me."

"No, thank you. Anyhow, Mason is excited for the baseball game later this week. Aren't you, buddy?" I try to refocus our attention to Mason.

"Yeah, but I wanted to go to a Sox game," Mason complains.

Logan and I look at one another with feigned shock.

"Whoa there, buddy," Logan begins and brings his hands out in protest.

I chip in, "You know there's only one baseball team in Chicago, right?"

Logan and I give one another a knowing look.

"We'll turn him to the good side, don't worry," Logan assures me.

After ordering more food and drinks, we enjoy dinner, mostly talking about Mason's day at camp where they learned about tornados and hurricanes. When Mason puts a game on his iPad, Logan and I exchange a glance, knowing we can now have simple adult conversation.

"Good day at work?"

"Yeah, surprised I made it out on time. I could easily put a few more hours in." Logan rubs a hand across his jaw. "You? Good day at work?"

I smirk to myself. "Yeah, can't complain. My boss is up to mischief, which has me slightly concerned." I push his foot away from me using my own ankle. It seems Logan decided to play footsie with my calf.

He grimaces. "I think you have a perfect boss who is a complete gentleman and only wants to ensure you go home *very* satisfied."

"Logan," I warn him with a way-too-playful voice.

"Seriously, though, can you spend the night this week? I need to cram in visiting Zoe again, plus finalizing a few transactions at work."

My jaw moves side to side. He'd asked me about this before we slept together. I had agreed, and to be honest, he genuinely seems to be serious. It makes sense.

"Sure, the guest room has a nice bed," I reply.

He gently shakes his head at my response and lets the back of his finger glide along his upper lip as he leans back in the booth.

"We'll see about that."

15

LOGAN

"Can I have ice cream?" Mason asks, jumping in front of me.

"Hmm, you already had enough at the game, I think you're set," I tell him as we walk along the street. Looking to my other side, I watch Sadie walking next to me in simplistic beauty wearing jeans and a Cubs shirt.

She gives me an agreeable look for giving my nephew a hard no.

"What about a cookie?" he tries his luck again.

This time Sadie delivers the bad news. "Sorry, Mase, but it's bedtime when we get home." She places her hands on his shoulders.

He groans, but we ignore him. It's already a little late since we were at a baseball game. It was perfect; Mason had a wide smile the whole time, and Sadie is adorably cute when she cheers for a homerun. It was nice having them both by my side. Even when I ran into people from my professional circle and I would do the socially correct conversation, my eyes kept wandering to Sadie who had a radiant smile as she helped ensure Mason had hot dogs to eat and pointed to the field and screen to explain the game.

This doesn't help my dilemma for the evening. I've asked Sadie to stay the night so I can leave super early in the morning. I wanted to offer her a bedroom choice, but I'm trying to respect her wishes.

My ego should be hurt that she put gentle brakes on us, but my ego is doing just fine. Mostly because I know she's struggling just as I am, trying to fight a good thing between us. She is trying to be the mature one for both of us. Kudos to her.

My shoulder grazes Sadie's as we walk along the sidewalk home. "You're okay taking him in the morning? I can see Zoe then before my meetings for the day."

"Sure, it's no problem."

"I'm not sure I have any normal food for breakfast in the house. This morning we were down to Fruity Pebbles—which aren't half bad."

She smiles. "Good choice, but I actually went to the supermarket this afternoon before picking up Mason. We—I mean, *you*—have toaster waffles and some healthier cereal. I'll pack his lunch in the morning."

This conversation is quite domestic, and for some reason, my body fights the warm and fuzzy feeling brewing somewhere inside me.

"Thanks."

The whole night, she has been trying to avoid eye contact. A few times, our gaze caught on one another, and it was pure smolder. Sexual tension on steroids, really.

I look at my nephew walking a few paces in front of us, and he seems far away enough that he can't hear, so I decide to put on my discretionary voice.

"So, you're sleeping in my bed, right?" I want to rile her. It's fun.

So much for being respectful. I'm an ass.

Sadie chuckles. "We have been over this. Not a great idea."

"Yet still you smile."

She stops and turns her body to me, and her look is cute. "Persistence is refreshing, but I just… I don't know."

For the first time, I can see her reluctance is because it's important to her. I touch her arm and encourage her to continue walking next to me.

She explains, "I'm not good with no-strings, you know, and since we're with one another daily, then it makes it even harder."

Normally, I don't think about these things. I don't let my feelings get involved when sex is the main driver. My feelings got involved once, and I got burned. I know where she's coming from, but I still don't want to let her escape that easily.

She already thinks I'm skirting the lines of being a player —has from the moment we met—and I debate about telling her that very few women even make it to my bed, as I normally stick to hotels, and morning afters are not my thing… except with her, it seems. But I know if I tell her the truth that I could be setting her expectations up, and I may not be able to deliver. I'm not her prince.

"Maybe you're right," is what I manage to say. "But I'm not sure what this is." Geez, honesty keeps creeping up on me today.

She side-glances at me in understanding.

Right on cue, we arrive at my building and head inside. We listen to Mason talk about the game as we ride the elevator up, but I can see he's beat.

Within ten minutes, I have him tucked in. Aware that Sadie is under my roof, I head to the living room, very well determined to pick up our conversation.

When I reach the living room, she's hovering over the hamster cage. I scratch the back of my head; I keep forgetting Mason brought that thing.

"Shall I open us a bottle of wine?" I ask, deciding to take step one of my plan of action for the evening.

"Uh, Logan, I think we have a problem."

I walk over to her and try to see what she's looking at. "What is it?"

She points to the hamster in the corner.

"Yeah, the hamster—forget his name. Snuffles, Bubbles…"

"Rumble *was* his name…" She peers at me while I check out the hamster who's a goner and register the news that my nephew's pet is roadkill.

I sigh and let my hands rub along my face. "This is fucking great." I'm not at all serious. It's the absolute last thing I need.

"Did you feed him?" she asks.

"I thought Mason was doing that?"

She scoffs at my answer. "He's seven, he may need a reminder or two."

"Crap. This will devastate him." My cartoonish-looking facial expressions take over as I stare at the dead hamster in the cage.

"Maybe… we could… swap him?" She looks at me with an equally funny face and cracked voice.

"As in get a new one and hope he doesn't notice?"

She nods.

Gosh, I love her devious side—it's hot.

"You think we can order online and it will be delivered

before breakfast?" I wonder half-seriously.

"Doubt that. Maybe there's a pet store still open. I mean, it is only eight-thirty, and this is a major US city."

I pull up my phone and decide to use my asshole boss move, phoning Jen.

"Sorry, but I have an SOS," I speak into my phone.

"You want me to send Sadie a basket already?" Jen asks on the other end.

I grit my teeth and step away from Sadie as I speak into my phone with a tight jaw. "No. I. Do. Not. Don't ask, but I need a hamster ASAP. I'll send you a photo of the guy; he needs to be identical," I explain before hanging up.

I return to the kitchen to see Sadie grabbing two wine glasses.

Ah, so she also needs something to take the edge off. She *will* drink with me tonight.

Thank you, hamster.

"Need alcohol now?" I confirm.

"Yes. I hope that thing doesn't have an evil spirit," she answers and visibly shivers at the thought.

"I can protect you… if you're in the proper setting tonight." I tip my head down and tilt my eyes up.

She brushes past my quip. "Do you always involve your assistant so late at night?"

I grab a bottle of wine from the fridge. "No, I can be a good boss. This was just an emergency."

A few minutes later, we're back at our usual spots on the couch with wine in hand. I'm beginning to believe this couch is almost an oasis in my living room. With Sadie on it, then I'm in a temporary escape from the world.

"You know it isn't healthy what we're doing. Mason should learn about the cycle of life, he's old enough to understand," she mentions as she sips her red wine, and the idea of her sweet lips mixed with the expensive French grapes makes me almost forget what she said.

"Hey, I'm following your lead on this one. Why did you suggest it if it goes against child psychology 101?"

Her lips quirk as she stares into her wine that she's swirling around the glass. "I just figured he has a lot going on now. He's worried about his mom and sisters. Rumble was not a team player and croaked on us at the worst possible time."

I look at her fondly; I like how she says *us*. "I agree, plus I don't have time for a hamster funeral; I'll hopefully close the Vey deal tomorrow."

I don't care about Sadie's boundaries; my fingers reach for hers to link with mine. Then I give them a tug to encourage her to move my way.

She does move closer. So much so that my arm can move around her to make this scene like a perfect setting from when I was fifteen and wanted to make out for the first time. Here I am, thirty-two and still ridiculously excited.

"Sadie."

"Logan." She gives me an inquisitive look.

"You're doing a damn good job behaving, but I don't like it." My forehead meets her own, and her skin feels like it's sizzling from my mere touch.

"I don't like it either, but it's the right thing to do. I mean, you sign my paycheck, and you have a lot going on."

I pull away for a second. "Is that what's bothering you? That I pay you?"

Her mouth slants into a half-smile. "Doesn't bother me enough. I mean, I was your fake fiancée and slept with you off the clock, so it's not like I'm a call girl," she jokes, and I love her humor, and absolutely one day we should play out that scenario.

"Most definitely you are not, but I would still love to see those hula hoop moves."

"I just… had a good time with you, a *really* good time, too good of a time, and that's the problem."

"You keep saying that. Elaborate ple—" My phone vibrates, and I know I need to take that. Hopefully it means the hamster gods have sent us a new hamster via Jen.

Holding a finger up to indicate to Sadie to wait, I keep my other hand interlinked with hers while I reach forward for the phone lying on the coffee table and answer.

"Hey, Jen. Really? You are amazing… great, thanks." I hang up and look at Sadie with relief. "Crisis averted; Rumble 2.0 will arrive here shortly."

She pokes my chest, and I grab her finger to keep it there. "This is my cue to go to sleep. You need to get rid of Rumble 1.0, clean the cage, and tell Rumble 2.0 that he is on strict orders to live. I hate hamsters, actually, so I think I will head to bed since I'm off the clock."

"And since you're off the clock, then you head to my bed?" I give her a stern eye and grin.

She shakes her head with a smile. "Not happening."

"A kiss?"

She stands, still entertained by my persistence. "Nope, I'm behaving."

Reluctantly, I let her hand go, and she walks halfway out of the living room before she turns to me.

"The guest room has a lock, right?"

"Unfortunately," I muse.

"Good, because I have plans… alone." She winks at me before disappearing.

I groan and rub my face in my hands. How is this my life, that she isn't in my bed because I have a seven-year-old and a dead hamster under my roof?

SADIE

A subtle feathery touch strokes my upper back as I mumble and squirm in the very comfortable guest bed. The bed is a perfect cloud of pillows, and the mattress is just firm enough. It took a solid hour of tossing and turning before I fell asleep, though, but I can't blame the bed. Logan Jax occupying my mind takes full credit for my inability to fall asleep.

"Sadie."

Am I dreaming? Is Logan's throaty morning voice in the room with me?

I quickly wake and turn to find the man of my recent fantasies sitting on the bed, dressed in his suit with a slick grin greeting me.

"Logan?" I rub my eyes.

"Trust me, say the word and I will make your wake-up so much better."

I blink at him. *This is real, right?*

He must pick up on the fact that I'm struggling to understand why he's here.

"I have to go but wanted you to know before Mason

wakes that the hamster problem has been completed, so fingers crossed he doesn't notice." Logan's fingers brush a few loose strands of my hair behind my ear.

To be honest, I'm beginning to think that if he has a few minutes to spare then he could possibly help me with a problem that I need relief from. My policy be damned.

"Oh right, the hamster. I should get up." I yawn. I forgot about that crisis.

But I don't move, nor does he stop stroking my hair. It feels relaxing, and my head dives into his hand to feel his palm rub against my cheek. I want that perfect skin with just enough roughness to smother my body.

I kiss his hand with a soft kiss and let my eyes peer up to his face, feeling a layer of heat spreading between my folds.

"You're not playing fair, Sadie." He groans, but his grin tells me that he doesn't mind.

"My apologies," I tell him one-toned.

The corner of his mouth hitches up, and his eyes give me a glint. "I swear to God, if we didn't have the issue of my nephew about to wake, I would take you so hard right now until the headboard slams against the wall."

"Sounds like you have a point to prove," I flirt. One hundred percent flirt.

He stands up from the bed and grumbles, with his eyes not leaving me. "I have to get out of here before I lose my goddamn mind."

I realize that I'm not playing fair when I see the zipper of his pants bursting at the seams. Throwing my legs out from the bed, I come to stand. I'm in shorts and a tank, but that's enough for Logan to hiss as he catches his breath, and I want to pounce on him.

Trying to think of another topic to save us from the predicament that we find ourselves in, my mind does a quick roll through a list of safe topics, and I blurt out, "Coffee." If it was a question or statement, I'm not sure, and my voice is uneven from the fact I'm about to drown in my own puddle of arousal.

He coughs into his hand. "Yeah, coffee... uhm... there's a pot in the kitchen."

"Great, thanks." Then I laugh to myself. "I guess we've never had coffee together." We were about to have a cup together the other day after morning sex, but life had other plans.

"A damn shame. We should change that, but I have to go... Another day." He looks at me, hopeful.

"Yeah, I would like that."

Coffee together is fine. Morning sex doesn't have to be a prerequisite.

––––––––

MASON DIDN'T NOTICE the hamster switch-up. To be honest, I didn't notice either. Rumble 1.0 and 2.0 look identical. After getting Mason ready for the day then dropping him off at camp, I decide to go for a walk and browse a few stores, as the summer sales are still going on and I should get a few outfits before I embark into the professional world. Hesitantly, I walk through Victoria's Secret and consider a few options for a scenario that absolutely should not happen.

I sigh loudly and pull my phone out and hit Emily's name on the screen while I stare aimlessly at a black lace number that is see-through everywhere, with strings as straps that would probably snap in an instant under Logan's strong touch.

Emily answers on the other end of the call. "Hey, Sadie. Everything okay?"

"No. It's horrible, absolutely horrible."

I can hear her laugh at me.

"I won't survive. I'm struggling," I add.

"Then you have your answer about what to do."

"Maybe I should switch perspectives and just go into this with the full understanding that it's only sex and fun," I declare with every morsel of confidence that I can manage to gather—and it's not a lot.

"Hmm, could be one approach. Except sometimes our minds and hearts can't separate fun and feelings. Again, I think you should see where it goes. Who knows, right? I mean, he's only your boss for like a month or so more. That's nothing. Even if you were considering quitting, then you wouldn't leave them hanging until they found someone else. I know you."

I bite my inner lip as my fingers stay firm on the hanger of the lingerie set. "I just —I can't figure out what intrigues me more. Logan in person when we talk or Logan when we're screwing each other's brains out."

"Newsflash, you can have both. Get to know them both. Or just let the mood lead you. Hey, have you ever considered that the reason you feel so strongly about all of this is because it's perfect chemistry and attraction? Maybe you didn't have that before and it's new. Heaven help us, but we all go through a hell of a lot of frogs before finding a prince."

I freeze and think about her words; she is on point today.

"But he needs a friend now. He has so much going on—"

"Sadie, I could strangle you. The man is thirty-two, worth a fortune, and runs a company. Something tells me he knows what he needs. He doesn't need you to make that decision for him. Sure, maybe he has a history with the ladies, but other than having a nephew staying with him, he's not waving any red flags. He's got his shit together. Maybe follow his lead."

My fingers release the hanger. "If I follow his lead then I'll end up in bed with him."

An almost evil laugh escapes from Emily. "Probably. By the way, where are you now? Shouldn't you be babysitting?"

"Mason is at camp until the afternoon. I was just checking out the sales."

"Oh yeah? Anything good?"

"A few. Victoria Secret has a good one."

Oh crap, I'm obvious.

"You know, for someone who wants to become home-maker of the year, something tells me you have a wild side in the bedroom."

"Anyone can have a wild side in the bedroom," I remind her. "Just like I know that you're no angel."

Emily chuckles at my response. "Considering you're eyeing lingerie, I think you have your answer of what you want." I can hear a smug grin on my friend's face.

Deep within me, I know she's right.

———

LOGAN IS LATE COMING HOME, so Mason is already asleep by the time he arrives. Logan strides in with confidence and a cheeky look, complete with bottle of champagne in hand.

I place my tablet on the coffee table before I hop up off the sofa and walk toward Logan with an amused look.

"You seem happy today," I comment.

His look at me is criminal, and in a quick move, his arm encircles me, and he pulls me close. I sink into the feeling when I should be stepping back and keeping my ground. But following his lead is also an option.

Our foreheads touch. "What are you doing? This isn't part of the plan," I remind him, but I'm not protesting anymore.

"It completely is. We said if I charm you that we can re-negotiate a particular term that I know you thoroughly enjoy."

"You said that, but that doesn't mean I agreed," I correct him. "What has you in such a good mood?"

His grin is wide and his mouth hovers around my neck and ear. I feel his hands moving around my hips. "So, dear *fiancée –*"

"Fake fiancée and an *ex*-fake fiancée at that," I correct him.

He growls softly into my neck. "The deal is done. William signed today."

My hands rest on his shoulders while I watch him and take in his words. I'm happy for him, he deserves this, and I must say it makes me slightly giddy that I played a minor role in all of this.

"That's great news!" I hug him, and he responds by lifting me up, tight to his body with my legs hanging straight. His body is so close to mine that it energizes me.

Setting me down, he kisses my forehead and lets the back of his hand stroke my cheek before he steps away to grab champagne glasses from the cabinet in the living room. "You'll stay and have a drink with me?"

"Of course, wouldn't want you to celebrate alone."

"You were part of it," he says as he twists the foil off the champagne.

The sound of the popping cork and the fizz of the champagne being poured is a relaxing soundtrack.

Logan hands me a glass as we stand in the middle of the room. Our glasses clink and eyes hold as we both drink. The buzz I feel isn't from the champagne, though, it's from his intense eyes and the feeling of his body close enough to touch.

"Congrats, it's been a big week for you." I smile.

Invading my personal space, he pulls me to him, and we join in the middle. I don't pull away—no, I enjoy being in his arms and drinking champagne too much.

"I would say so. New nieces, closed a billion-dollar deal, slept with a beautiful woman and will do so again."

I choke on my drink.

Maybe it's adrenaline, or this is just cocky Logan, but his confidence is strong and energy high tonight. His fingertips on my sides guide me to walking back until my ass hits the edge of the dining table. Setting his flute of champagne down, he grabs mine and does the same. Watching him just sends exhilaration through me. He's always in control and leading the way. It's a turn-on, so incredibly sexy and enticing.

His hands grab my legs, and he wraps them around his waist before his hands come to frame my face.

Bad choice on my part today for wearing a skirt. This is not helping me keep my guard up. "What are you doing?" My eyes draw a line up and down his body, yet I can't help a slight grin from forming on my face.

"We should celebrate properly."

"Logan," I purr because my body is disloyal to my brain.

"There's only one thing I want tonight, so let's make it happen." His voice is determined. "Don't tell me to stop," he warns as he pulls my body tightly to his, and my arm entwines around his neck. I feel his hard erection press into me, causing a throbbing feeling running strongly between my legs.

"Don't stop." I barely manage to whisper an answer, but I'm done fighting this attraction between us.

Yet again, I didn't even last a week this time.

His mouth slants, and in an instant, our mouths seal

together. His taste is addicting, and the champagne on his firm and commanding lips doesn't help, the remnants of his five-o'clock shadow slightly rough around my mouth.

He demands my tongue with his own, and he gets it. I'll give him whatever he wants, and I have a few ideas of my own.

Our kiss is long and sensual as all sense of time evaporates.

Why does this have to feel so good?

His hands hold my face firmly in place so he can kiss me with force. It flips a switch on in me, and I desperately want more.

"I think I might take you right here on the table," he murmurs into my neck.

"I don't care where, just please." *Yeah*, I desperately need this before I explode.

We're suddenly like two animals attacking each other, with hands roaming and our kisses running hard.

"Touch me," he demands.

My hand moves between us to find his impressive erection straining against the zipper of his pants.

"You feel good."

"It'll feel better inside you."

A hand slides up my thigh, his strong perfect hand. He needs to move fast, I want him to touch me, take care of me.

Click.

We both freeze in our tracks. Our eyes move to the side as our mouths stay intact. Very quickly we realize that in three seconds a little boy is going to interrupt us.

In a flash, we pull apart. Logan steps back and runs his hand through his hair while I straighten my clothes.

Mason comes to the middle of the living and dining area with his hand rubbing his head.

"Hey, buddy, everything okay?" I ask and realize I must look like a disheveled human because *I am*.

"No, the alien will come for me," Mason moans as he looks to the floor and walks to his uncle.

My eyes shoot to Logan with an I-told-you-so grin.

"Is it because you watched that movie with your uncle?" I cross my arms.

The little boy nods.

Logan has a tight-mouthed grin. "How about I take you back to bed."

"NO! Can I sleep in your room tonight?" Mason pleads.

Logan looks deflated, as if the kid punched the air from his uncle's lungs.

I offer a reassuring smile. "It's okay. I need to go anyways."

Logan mouths the word *no* to me, but I just shake my head.

Half an hour later, I text Logan to let him know that I'm home.

MR. CHARMER

No, come back.

Uh, you have a guest in your bed

The wrong guest.

It's maybe for the best. You had some strong plans of action for tonight.

Trust me, that wasn't even a preview.

Night, Logan.

Night, beautiful... meet me at my office for early lunch tomorrow.

I smile at that sentence.

You're missing a question mark.

It's not a question.

He inserts a winking emoji.
And without thought, I answer:

Okay. See you tomorrow.

Arriving at Logan's office, I feel a wave in my stomach as I straighten the skirt of my dress, a simple olive-green summer dress that ends just above my knees. Jen smiles at me from behind her desk.

"Hey, Sadie, how are you today? Heard about the hamster issue," Jen says as she finishes typing something on her laptop.

"Hi. Yeah, you worked some magic to make that happen. How did you do it?" I'm still slightly astonished at the quick turnaround.

Jen loudly hits the enter key then focuses her attention on me. "Simple. I told the pet store that we would pay triple plus a hefty tip for them to deliver the hamster. Money does wonders sometimes. Come on, he's expecting you."

I follow her as she walks toward the hall to Logan's office —the only office with full privacy, I duly note. Something tells me that Jen is one of *those* personal assistants. The special kind who is a keeper of secrets and is probably totally aware I've already screamed Logan's name while lying underneath him, but she won't let on she knows that fact.

"Thanks," I answer.

I swallow and internally question myself again why I've agreed to show up. It's completely ridiculous, because I would consider myself someone who stays true to their standpoint. But with Logan Jax, I am a woman under a spell. He's persuasive, and we have this pull that can't be denied, and it won't let me look away.

My heart rate picks up, I can feel it in my chest. I swear I can hear my pulse in my ears. Every step closer to his office is upping the eagerness I have for him.

What *am* I doing here? A chat? Lunch? Sex on his desk?

The moment I arrive in the doorway to his office, I see him leaning back in his chair with his feet on his desk, talking on his cell phone. He doesn't have a suit jacket on, instead the sleeves of his dress shirt are rolled up. Logan crooks his hand toward him and instructs us that it's okay to come in as he simultaneously tells whoever is on the phone that he has to go. I don't think he even gives them a chance to say goodbye before he hangs up.

Jen looks between Logan and me then clears her throat. "Right, well, I'll leave you two. You have a reservation at Cups and Jars in twenty minutes," she reminds him before pivoting, and I see she has a cunning look on her face. This could possibly be her warning flare to me that I'm in trouble, but I already established that the moment I met this man.

I hear the click of the door, but I don't look behind me. I assume it's closed. It wouldn't matter, as I'm too focused on the man in front of me whose perfect blue eyes are set on me.

While we have a moment of silence, it changes in a flash.

He springs out of his chair and nearly charges for me. The moment he stops in front of me, his sweltering look comes on. His hands firmly cradle my head, and before I even have a chance to greet him, he beats me to the punch by greeting me with a deep warm kiss on my mouth.

It's the type of kiss that has you melting. And I do. I melt into him. My hands slide around his waistcoat, pulling him tightly to me as we prolong the kiss that will leave me completely breathless. Our murmurs sound… blissful.

I already feel disappointed when his lips gently pull away.

"Sadie, Sadie, Sadie, what am I going to do with you?" he whispers, full of faux-malice as his thumb gently rubs my bottom lip.

"Hello to you too."

He smiles, now that we have a moment to take in the fact that we're in front of one another.

"So," it drags from my mouth. "What are we doing?" I give him a questionable look.

He grabs my hand and kisses it. *What a gentleman.*

"We have reservations for this lunch spot nearby, but right now, the hotel on the corner is looking like a great option." His look is purely wicked.

"Lunch sounds good if your desk isn't an option," I retort.

His eyes narrow in on me. "Oh, trust me, it could be an option."

I step away to break the heat we're creating in the air.

"But… what are we doing?" I ask again as he grabs his phone from his desk, and his eyes whip up to mine with a look that tells me he's been waiting for this.

Walking around his desk, he perches on the ledge and encourages me with his hands to come to him.

I do, and he pulls me closer then encircles his arms around me.

"We're not fighting this attraction between us. I don't have anything else to say, because I don't know what happens except that I enjoy being with you."

What he's saying isn't disheartening, mostly because it isn't a surprise—he can't offer commitment.

Still, I reluctantly admit, "I'm not sure I can do no-strings if that's what you want."

His hand comes to hold my face in his palm. "It would be kind of hard since I see you every day. I'm not promising the moon but enjoying one another."

"You are technically my boss."

"Technicality."

"It doesn't bother you that I'm younger?"

"It's a fantasy come true. Besides, eight years isn't that much," he assures me.

"It doesn't bother me." I know all my questions were a stalling tactic, when inside, I know I've already agreed to fun.

"So tonight, you'll sleep in my bed?" he volleys.

I laugh and playfully slap his shoulder. "Absolutely not, considering Mason interrupted us last night. In no way are we risking that."

He frowns. "Maybe the hotel is a good idea, we can order room service."

The tips of my fingers touch each side of his face. "I wouldn't be opposed to the idea, but lunch with you in a public place to keep you in line sounds good. But maybe…"

What I'm about to say excites me and it arouses me. It makes me feel proud that I'm taking risks.

"I could help you right now." It comes out slowly from my mouth as my eyebrows raise.

He growls into my neck before looking into my eyes again. "Sadie, I want nothing more than to have you on your knees for me, watching you try and take my big cock deep in your throat and then have you swallowing my come. But I need you lying in a bed so I can take you several ways."

"Promise me you'll let me another time then?" My voice is feathery.

"I don't need to promise that. You can do whatever you want to me. Just like I will do whatever I want to you. You will enjoy it. Now, let's get the hell out of my office before I change my mind and bend you over my desk for the whole office to hear."

We grin at one another, and I think it's more because we are completely satisfied with our answers.

———

WE WALK into the restaurant and there is a busy lunchtime rush. Mason jars sit on tables with candles, farm-to-table food whizzing by on plates, and this place is almost romantic. The whooshing of the revolving door sounds as we arrive inside, but immediately Logan stops in his tracks, and I nearly crash into him.

Stepping to the side, I notice his face has gone blank and his body stills. Turning to where he's looking, I see a woman standing in front of us with a tight, blond-haired bun, perfect make-up, and a pant suit.

An unnerving silence surrounds us, and I'm not sure what's going on. They definitely know each other.

"It's been a while," the woman says, breaking the silence.

"It has," he replies.

I have a feeling that they've forgotten that I'm here.

There's a pause before the woman continues, "How have you been? How's Zoe?"

Logan scratches his cheek; a habit I've noticed he does when slightly nervous. He isn't a man who gets that nervous either. "I'm good. Zoe just had twins actually, now she's a mother of three."

"Oh, that's great news. Guess the Jax twin gene is in full force."

I feel completely uncomfortable and begin to look around the room, but my eyes catch the woman again, and she notices, causing her to attempt to smile at me.

"Well, I will let you two have your lunch. I'm in town visiting my folks; they're with my daughter now."

"Right, I heard. Congrats, and thanks, we do have lunch reservations," he states.

"Take care."

"You too."

She leaves, and he stands there while I remain utterly confused.

Logan interlaces our hands. "Let's get some lunch. The BLT is great." He moves on like the last excruciating two minutes didn't just happen.

I squeeze his hand. "Uhm, everything okay? Who was that?"

His bottom jaw clenches. "My ex-wife."

LOGAN

"So, you haven't seen her in ten years?" Sadie asks me in complete astonishment. We're sitting at our corner table, side by side in the booth. The waiter has already delivered my scotch. Sadie declined the needed drink kick since she has to pick-up Mason at two pm.

When Sadie asked, I was honest. I haven't seen Kate in ten years, and it only seems fitting that I speak about my ex-wife with the woman who I should be thrusting into in this very moment.

"No need, but it's okay, we're history. I just didn't expect to see her. I've managed not to run into her for this long."

Sadie gently touches my arm. "Don't you want to talk to her more? That was, well, a bizarre conversation."

"Really, we have nothing to talk about. She's married now with a kid, just like she always wanted." I know this because Zoe mentioned once she'd heard via her old high-school friends.

There's a pause, but I know the interrogation is coming.

"Can I ask why it didn't work? And the real reason, not the paper version about how it wasn't meant to be."

I look at her, and her sparkly eyes invite me to open up. This isn't me. I don't talk in detail about these things, yet with her, I don't think twice. I take in a deep breath. "There was one time in my life that Zoe and I didn't speak. It was the fourteen months that I was with Kate. They were best friends, and even though I knew it was a dangerous move, Kate and I were young and had fun. One day, we decided to elope, and it didn't pan out well. We soon realized that other than having fun, we weren't that compatible."

"How so?" She encourages me by rubbing my arm.

"Right away she wanted a baby, and that was nowhere on my radar. I wouldn't budge on that. She wanted a house in the suburbs, complete with kids and a dog. I wanted to climb up the professional ladder, but in honesty, that was just one of the many issues."

Sadie nervously bites her lip. "Your sister was mad?"

I look at Sadie more intently, trying to figure out why she hasn't run away yet at the craziness that my life throws her way. "Zoe was furious. She kept telling me that I would only screw up her friendship with her best friend and, well…" I tip my scotch glass. "Zoe was right, and now they don't speak anymore."

"And you feel bad about that?"

"Don't feel great about it, but it's water under the bridge now."

"Until you run into the boat again. Are you sure you're okay?"

I take her hand and give her an appreciative look. "Sadie, I am absolutely okay. Sure, it caught me off guard running into her. But I don't regret ending it, and I don't ever think I should have tried. She ended up where she was supposed to, and I ended up where I was supposed to. I'm not husband or father material."

Sadie nods, and I'm smart enough to know that her mind must be working in overtime.

"I promise," I assure her, and it's the truth.

"I guess I get it. I mean, my ex and I were together for the same amount of time as you and Kate. I also feel completely content with how it ended and where I am now," she proclaims.

I don't like thinking of her with anyone. I've claimed her, and I'll confirm it again next time too.

I am not a caveman.

"You didn't mention." My face remains neutral.

She gives me a half-smile. "He was an immature asshole, and you, well… you are the opposite. Most certainly more dominating, more skilled, and you get me."

"Please continue that list in my favor," I smirk.

"We both have histories; yours may be a bit longer in length in terms of partners, but I'm not naïve, Logan."

"Never thought you were. In fact, you're more mature than me on some days. But still, you need to listen to me because I am older and wiser." I'm only half-teasing.

Her look remains slightly wary.

It dawns on me that we've had some deep conversations, and I'm not complaining either.

The waiter interrupts us with our food, and we get settled with our plates and start to eat. This BLT sandwich is exactly what I need today, and I like the way Sadie steals one of my fries since she ordered soup and salad.

"So, you're a fry stealer."

The way she nibbles on the fry is torture. The things I can't wait for her to do.

"I am. What are you going to do about it?"

Pure torture.

"How about tomorrow, I move some meetings around so I

can be home for a long lunch, and you meet me there?" I propose, and it's a smart idea on my part since my nephew is away at camp. We would have the place to ourselves, and the sun hits my room perfectly midday to watch her as she climaxes.

"I could make it work possibly. Why do I have the feeling actual food is not on the menu?" She leans into my arm.

"If you're a good girl then it can be arranged."

———

THE NEXT DAY, I arrive home fully ready.

After our lunch yesterday, it was oddly calm between us. The whole situation almost seemed effortless, meant to be, and that's just insanity. When I returned from work, I watched Sadie help Mason with his workbook before stealing a kiss goodbye when my nephew wasn't looking. Today, well… today has been on my mind since the moment we had to cut short our morning in bed the other weekend.

Walking into the kitchen, Sadie—who is in a short, summery, pink cotton dress with easy-to-pull straps—is busy putting something back in the fridge. I'm not even going to ask what she's doing. I slide my arms around her from behind, and she hums a sound as she molds to my body.

"This isn't the room you should be waiting in," I remind her.

"You didn't send me instructions," she taunts me. Next time she will get a very detailed text of commands prior to meeting.

I squeeze her ass and begin to pull her with me toward my room. Her giggle makes me smile as my arms stay around her while I walk her forward until we're in the middle of my room where full sun shines through my big windows.

All morning I've debated how I'm going to take her, and I know just how.

"On the bed," I whisper into her ear, and I feel her shiver from my command.

You know a woman is magical when, without debate, she proceeds to follow your request.

I walk to the bed but stop. Without instruction she kneels and faces me.

"Let's get this off you." She bites her lip, and her face has a seductive pout as she unbuttons my shirt.

"Good idea."

A wave of pressure shoots down to my swelling cock as her hands unbuckle me then pull the zipper of my pants down. I've got to keep it together, but already I want to plunge into her.

"Turn around," I demand.

The moment she does, I pull her flush to me, her back to my front. Her sudden jolt and sound of enjoyment is so encouraging. Swiftly, I hike the bottom part of her dress to her hips and let my knuckles gently run a line from the side of her knee up her thigh. An avenue of pure silky skin and heat.

My erection presses into her back, and it makes her flinch then let out a sweet little sound that I wish I could record. *Maybe next time*.

"Have you been wet for me all morning, waiting for me?"

"Yes." She's eager as her hand meets mine and urges me to touch her between her legs.

"You want to show me?" I breathe into her ear.

"Let me show you."

She brings my fingers under the very thin piece of fabric covering her smooth flesh. I can already smell the sweet arousal, and the warm thickness coats my fingers as I run my digits along her slick heat. Her hips arch into my touch.

"Patience, baby," I remind her.

She whimpers when I remove my hand and instead bring my hands to pull her dress straps down and lower her dress, so all the fabric is bunched above her waist. She has no bra on, and I like that she came prepared.

My fingers find her nipples and they gently pinch those beautiful hard pebbles. I kiss her neck as she moans.

"You like that?"

She murmurs an agreement.

"You like when I touch your beautiful tits?"

"Logan, yes, you're making me so wet," she rasps.

Keeping one hand on her breast, the other returns to feel her slit, and hot damn, she *is* wetter.

"I don't know what to do to you first—taste you or see how many fingers I can slip inside of you." My finger skirts the edge of her opening.

My straining cock is getting painful and full. Her hand wandering behind her back and gripping my dick isn't helping the situation.

"You know what I want," she reminds me.

I drop my hands and grip her shoulders to turn her, our eyes meeting with blazing desire.

"I do know. Now open your mouth."

Nothing is better than a woman saying she wants to give you oral—no, I lie. Better is when they *remind* you that they want to give you oral.

She moves back to sitting on the mattress and shimmies her body closer to where I'm still standing with knees against the bed. My hardened cock plays and brushes along her nipples, which makes her throw back her head with a moan as her hair falls everywhere.

It seems to set off a sense of urgency in her, and she quickly brings her mouth to my tip as her hand holds me firmly at the base. The wetness of her mouth soon covers my length, inch by inch, before she hits the end of her limit. I grab her hair and guide her as she slides her tongue and thrusts her mouth around me, occasionally hitting her gag reflex, but then adjusting her rhythm.

There's an inferno between my legs happening, and I just want to let go because it hurts so much. I need the release, and her talented mouth does not disappoint.

"Sadie, be careful, I'll come," I have to admit.

Adding another amazing trait to Sadie Bay, she just takes me deeper and firmer, her eyes peering up to me, giving me the okay. She wants me in her mouth, and a few thrusts later, I stiffen, muscles tense, and relief unleashes into her as my body goes rigid. Still she doesn't let me go. I feel her swallow, and she's making me want her more by the minute.

She pulls away with a satisfied look, but already my cock feels lost without her. Her eyes are almost watering from how deep she took me.

"Mmm, you taste good."

I like it when I'm control during sex, but this woman is throwing me off. She is surprise after surprise.

"Take off your dress, and I want you on your hands and knees. Let me see your ass."

She smiles and quickly pulls her dress up and off before turning slowly, with intention, to all fours, and her beautiful ass is on full display.

I grab the thin black lace of her panties and pull them down with haste. Dropping to the bed on my own hands and knees, I crash my mouth onto her opening and taste her, very sweet on my tongue, making my erection re-emerge.

I feast on her until I have her quivering and she fully spasms. Only when she returns from her orgasm do I move us on to the finale.

I watch her touch herself while I grab a condom, but my eyes can't leave her. She has me in a trance, and a glimmer of something more flashes in my head—but her inviting eyes bring me back to the moment, and I return to her. I guide her back, so she's sitting on my lap reverse-cowgirl style as I sit on my knees.

Sadie circles her hips around my cock, and I like that she is purposely putting on a little show.

"Slide right onto me, baby." I encourage her, and she obeys, with the heat of her pussy surrounding my cock. She moves her hips and pelvis, up and down.

"That's it, baby," I praise her.

"Oh… oh… Logan."

I reach for her clit to rub, and my other hand cups her breast, and these actions make her move faster on me.

"I need you deeper," she gasps.

I *need* to be in her deeper. I need to fill her to the hilt.

We quickly re-adjust our position until we're lying on our sides, staring at one another with my one leg tucked between her thighs as I bring her leg high across my hip, creating a wide opening.

Our feral actions from before calm down, and we move slower while I thrust deeply into her and our eyes lock. I move my arm underneath her and pull her to me as my other hand rests on her hip. We move in rhythm, with our mouths meeting for a searing kiss before her lips rest on my neck and she moans into my skin.

I need her closer, and I pull her tighter to me.

We're as close as we can get. But I need more.

I kiss her forehead. She continues to gasp on each pump I give her as we race towards a climax.

"Come with me," I nearly groan as that familiar pressure leading to a release approaches.

"Yes, yes, yes," she sounds off.

We spiral, we shake, we release.

Then we lie there holding each other as my hands squeeze her ass but tenderly in a smooth circle.

Her mouth forms a smile so breathtaking, with her fingers drawing lazy designs on my cheeks as I wilt inside her. We're both trying to steady our breathing, but we're lost.

In the moment.

In each other.

We kiss, and it pains me that I need to go take care of the condom. God, I want to fill her up without a layer between us. Why is my mind thinking these thoughts?

"Be right back." I kiss her forehead.

I return a minute later to Sadie lying completely spent in my bed. And I understand.

I have to head back to the office soon, but not after a little more time with her. Lying next to her, she cuddles into my chest and I wrap an arm around her.

"Is there a way we can stop time and just do that again and lie here all day?"

I smile at her idea. "I wish, but no. I should go shower, but I want your smell and taste on me for the rest of the day."

"You can be crass… but I like it."

"No, crass would be me telling you I want to fill you up, so you feel me inside you all day."

I look down at her eyes staring up at me, the size of saucers, and she has a beaming smile with a slight shake of her head. She laughs, and it makes her neck arch forward, and I use the opportunity to kiss her skin with a little teeth action.

The moment grows peacefully quiet as I look at her underneath me, and I want more of this. I'm not a cuddler, but for her I could be.

"So, what's my name on your phone now?"

She smiles. "Trouble and Charmer, I'm too scared to change it."

And while I should take that as a simple joke, I hear the undertone of hesitation in her. She needs the reminder because she's unsure if I'll hurt her, and truthfully, I don't have an answer.

I t's been four days since we had incredible lunchtime sex. We keep it completely professional when Mason is around—and he's around a lot. Hence why it's been four days. Luckily for us, the heavens granted Logan and me a three-hour window while Mason is at a birthday party for someone from his class last year.

Logan pushing into me from behind as we lie embraced is a holy way to spend a Sunday. My leg is draped over his hip behind me as he hits every inch inside me. He spoons me from behind, and he coaxes my mouth open with his thumb.

"We need to teach you to be quiet," he whispers in my ear. "I love that you're vocal, but I need you to be quieter so I have more opportunities to fuck you."

It just makes me moan more as I suck his thumb.

"Sadie, I'm not playing around." He pulls his thumb out before something else is placed in my mouth.

He is… something.

The taste of my wet satin panties fills my mouth to block my sounds as he tenderly kisses my shoulder and continues to pump inside me. This whole scene is erotic yet gentle, especially as he interlinks our right hands, and his mouth doesn't leave my skin. Soft shoulder kisses are my melting point.

My muffled moans go soft, as I'm trying to prove a point to him, but our bodies continue to move together.

"You feel so good around my cock. So wet and warm."

I need his mouth on mine, and I could easily take the fabric from my mouth, but I want him to do it when he approves that I have passed his test.

Our eyes meet, and they're saying something, but neither of us have figured out what. It makes him move differently inside of me; he slows down the pace, makes his thrusts longer.

His thumb strokes my cheek before he removes the fabric. "So beautiful."

Everything inside me is intensifying, and he must sense it because his mouth covers my own as he pulls me closer, and our joined hands move to my stomach. I love the sound of his cock slipping in and out.

Coming with him this time has me feeling like I'm floating, blind and light. As I come down from the climax, he's with me there. Logan doesn't loosen our embrace as he comes down too.

We lie staring at the other, and he stays inside me.

"I can sneak into the guest room now when you spend the night. We just keep you quiet." He kisses me.

"Hmm." I love moaning when his mouth is on me, even if it's just a kiss.

"But I want you in my bed," he states again. He slips out of me, but immediately inserts a finger inside of me before dragging it out.

His satisfied grin forms as he brings the finger with my come to my mouth. I suck, our eyes not parting. *Mmm.*

His mouth dives into my neck, and he speaks against my

skin. "Sadie, you're a dirty girl, and I'm not going to let you shower now."

I laugh and interlace our hands as I relax into the mattress. "You weren't going to anyway."

He moves to his side and props his head up with a bent arm. "Nope."

On our sides, we look at one another, our interlaced fingers dancing. I like the way our fingers meet.

"What are you smiling at?" He gives me a sheepish look.

"Nothing."

He kisses my forehead in an affectionate way.

I'm not complaining about our mid-afternoon trysts, I just keep needing to remind myself what this is.

Enjoying one another. Nothing more.

"So, is this how you normally spend your Sundays?"

Logan lets his fingertips glide along my arm. "You mean with a beautiful young woman who sometimes calls me boss lying in my bed?"

I playfully slap him.

He answers seriously now. "No, actually. I don't bring women here."

My eyes meet his, and I'm surprised by his statement. "Why is that?"

We shift in the bed so I can lie on my side, and I can't help but touch his chest.

"I haven't had time for anything but fun, and I prefer not to make it complicated."

"You don't like complication, yet here I am in your bed." I have to smile at him, giving him the reminder.

"You have a key to my home; you're here anyway," he tries to justify.

"For now, yes. Don't you one day want a woman waiting

for you when you get home from a grueling day at the office?" I know I'm poking him, but I can't help it.

"I don't know. I tried it once, and it didn't pan out well. Divorce does a funny thing to people." He doesn't look at me, and I begin to wonder if I'm prodding a bear.

"You were young then. I'm not sure you can compare."

"I was around your age, oh wise one. Now tell me, does Sadie Bay want a man waiting for her when she gets home from helping little children?" He squeezes me closer.

I have no problem with honesty. "I do. I want all of that. Husband, kids, and even a little puppy. Haven't decided about the house in the suburbs yet."

"Shouldn't you millennials be breaking away from tradition?"

I scoff. "Well, I mean, I think it's great women have options now in terms of career and family, but that's not me. I don't want to be my mother who worked non-stop. Women can balance both, but I don't think I can. I want to actually see my kids and cook dinner for the family, the upbringing I didn't have. In fact, if there were a university for how to become a housewife, then I would've attended it."

He looks at me as my eyes peer up to him. "You're joking with me, right?"

I shake my head no. "I enjoy what I studied, but I'm not sure I see myself in a lifetime of academia or working full-time."

"Hmm. So, what's your plan until you find Mr. Right?"

I shrug a shoulder. "Focus on the summer. Find an apartment before my new job starts and try to keep my current boss in line." My eyebrow cocks up when I look at him.

Logan quickly flops me to my back and cages me under him. "I think your boss is keeping his nanny in line."

"Oh yeah? I didn't notice," I feign with a mischievous smile.

"Didn't notice?" He gives me a warning look.

"No. Should I have noticed something *big*?" I tease him.

He tickles me immediately which makes me laugh and squirm under him, begging him to stop.

"Sadie, don't you even start. I might need to prove a point to you." His hand slides down my stomach to my thigh, then moves up but stops just on the outskirts of where I want him to touch me.

"I'll behave, I promise."

His eyes move up and down, as if he's assessing me, but then he kisses me, and it almost feels like it's full of purpose. I kiss back, and when we pull away, he kisses my nose and my forehead.

"Mason will need to be picked up soon," I remind him. "Then probably fed too."

Logan growls as he rolls out of bed and finds some clothes on the floor to put on.

"I'll order pizza or something," he says as he tugs his shirt down over his body.

I laugh at his suggestion. "I am positive Zoe would go through the roof. Mason probably had birthday cake at the party and now pizza. Let me check what's in your fridge, and I'll leave something for you guys."

Logan walks to the bed, grabs my arm, and tugs me up to him. His fingertips rest on my cheeks. "Stay for dinner."

"Not a smart move. He'll wonder why I'm here if not to babysit him," I remind him.

"Okay, then why don't you pick him up, and we pretend you're babysitting today. I'll give you my keys to the car," he jokes, but he's also serious.

It just makes me shake my head with a grin. "Can't happen. I can't drive your car."

He looks at me puzzled. "You don't drive?"

"I drive. Just not stick shift, and I'm positive your classic Aston Martin isn't an easy ride."

His eyes bug out. "Whoa, this I will not allow. You've never driven stick shift?"

I shake my head no.

"Well, that's about the change." He pulls me off the bed, and I quickly find clothes. Logan is up to something.

———

"Stop laughing at me. I'm trying!" I say for what feels like the tenth time. Logan's eyes haven't left me. His hand stays firmly on mine to help me guide the shifting of gears.

"You're doing well. *Considering…*"

"Really, please can we pull over? This is freaking me out. There's traffic!" I'm not exactly calm.

"It's fine, put your foot on the clutch, we're moving to second gear. I'll help you."

I do as he says, and I swear I nearly hit a car, but Logan remains calm, and he has a fixed grin on his face.

"Please, can we stop?" I beg.

"Relax, we're almost there, and then we can switch," he reminds me.

After what feels like forever, but in reality is two minutes, we park near the place Logan needs to pick up Mason. The moment the engine is off, we look at one another and both start to laugh hysterically.

"See, that wasn't bad," he says, giving me a look that's kind of adorable.

"I guess it wasn't."

"A little excitement is good for your heart rate."

"I thought I had that earlier today in your bed," I refute, which earns me a respectable grin.

"I deliver excitement in many ways, Sadie." His voice almost sounds like he's reprimanding me in a playful manner.

A loud exhale escapes me. "You'll drive back? I'll take the El back since I want to stop by a bookstore."

Logan leans in to kiss me, and he says, "Sure," against my lips. "I had a good time, Sadie."

"Me too." A *really* good time. Every day with him that feeling grows.

That isn't bad, but it isn't great, considering he isn't a commitment kind of guy.

We both have a soft smile, and I wonder what he's thinking. I feel like there's something floating in his head, and it has been all day. Neither of us says anything.

After getting out of the car, we both wait, leaning against his silver car.

"It's his last week of camp this week, right?" Logan double-checks with me.

"Yeah, and then he's home full-time. I guess until Zoe is settled with the twins at home, right?"

"Yep. I'm sure you have a full schedule planned for him already, but maybe I'll try and take a few days off." Logan lets a hand glide through his hair.

"Sounds good. Just tell me when, since I guess I won't be needed then."

He re-angles his body towards me. "*Actually*, I was thinking of taking Mason up to Wisconsin for a few days. He would like it."

I touch his arm. "He'll absolutely love it."

"Come with?" His tone is firm, as if it isn't an invitation, but a command.

"Oh, I…"

"You technically agreed already."

"But that was before I slept with you. Not sure it would be a good idea." I begin to play with my hair out of a nervous habit then bring my hair up into a ponytail.

"It's no different than when you're at my place," he reminds me.

"Kind of true, but I don't know. Let me think about it." The stakes feel higher this time.

Logan nudges my arm with his. "You could do your own thing while I take him fishing, then when he goes to sleep, well… I'm sure I can think of something we can do."

I shake my head at him. "First, Mason is smart. He'll wonder why I'm there when his uncle isn't working and is perfectly capable of taking care of him. Two, are you literally asking me to come or is it your dick asking me to come?" I'm not sure if I'm offended or amused.

It makes him grin. "It's me asking." He seems honest and serious.

"I'll think about it, okay?"

He nods slowly in agreement.

It's fun. It's fun. It's only fun.

20

LOGAN

"What is this rejuvenated look on your face?" Cole asks as he indicates to the barman for the same drink as me—specialty beer from Holland.

It's a quick after-work mid-week drink at a new bar that popped up in recent weeks. Hanging industrial lights, acoustic music, and artsy glasses—the place is clearly aiming for trendy.

"I look exactly like I did the last time you saw me." I take a sip of the hoppy brew.

"No, my friend. You look like a man who is getting properly fucked." Cole grins.

I try to avoid his gaze, but then can't help but raise my shoulder up toward my ears.

"Let's talk about the dip in the stock market, shall we?" I suggest, to steer us away from this topic of conversation.

But because he's an asshole, he doesn't relent. "You and Sadie are at it like rabbits?"

"Come on, I'm not getting into this. I want to get home for dinner, and this conversation with you feels like it might turn into unsolicited advice."

Cole's drink arrives and he takes a sip from the bottle. "You mean, get home for dinner with your nanny and nephew. In other words, playing house?"

I look at him, taken aback by his statement. "It isn't like that."

"So, you're not excited to be getting home for dinner?"

I mean, Sadie is a great cook, and the last few days, I have enjoyed reading with Mason. Having someone who you can kiss waiting for you in your kitchen isn't that bad either.

"It's stir-fry night." Why did I just say that like it was the highlight of my day? Maybe because… it is.

Cole lets a deep laugh escape. "Wow. Logan Jax is getting domesticated."

I don't appreciate my friend's tone. "Not sure it's that, considering Sadie is there to care for Mason."

"And when the kid goes to sleep?"

"We are perfectly behaved." …Except the other night when we managed a quickie in the kitchen since she came prepared and wasn't wearing any panties under her dress.

"What happens when Mason goes back to Zoe's? When Sadie is no longer the nanny always waiting for you at home?"

It feels like cold water being thrown at me, and I can't figure out why.

"Well, that's still a little while off. At least a few weeks, then I'll need to see."

"Christ, tell me you're not going to send her fruit." Cole tips his head to the side to study me.

"Nah… I'm not going to send her fruit," I admit, and it's the truth.

There's a long break in our conversation.

"Logan, could it be that you *really* enjoy being around her?" Cole looks around the bar as he asks that.

"I do enjoy being around her. I mean, not many women would agree to be my temporary fiancée," I say casually.

When Cole chokes on his beer, I remember that I never told him about that little detail.

"Come again? What did you just say?"

I smile to myself. "She agreed to play along to be my fiancée to land a client."

"And she needed to be your fiancée? A fake girlfriend wouldn't have done the trick?" He looks at me, skeptical.

"Fair point, but she was all game."

Cole grins. "Sounds like you've met your match."

"Maybe, but I don't think I'm the guy she needs in the long run. She wants it all with someone, and she deserves that. Whoever wins her heart will be a lucky guy." And the thought of her with someone else makes me want to vomit slightly. It's a horrible image. It's enough to make me question how to convince her to become a nun or something.

"That lucky guy is maybe you," Cole shoots out.

I give him side-eye. "I'm not taking advice from you. I don't exactly see someone on your arm."

"Yeah, because I don't have a good-looking nanny waiting for me at home with homecooked food and probably a hot-as-fuck summer dress—"

"Hey! Watch it," I warn him.

We both take a drink from our bottles.

"I fucking love this. My best friend is falling for the nanny, and he may actually settle down."

I take a sip of my beer, trying to get his words to leave my head.

———

I MANAGED to get Cole's words out of my head for the most part before I returned home last night. Instead, I relished dinner with Sadie and Mason. After Sadie left, Mason and I played a few rounds of Jenga—and the kid has skills.

Today, I'm visiting my sister. Everyone is doing better on that front; the babies can even be with my sister and will probably all get to go home this weekend. I asked Sadie to meet me at the hospital with Mason. I'm early, so I arrive to my sister holding one of the twins. I couldn't say which one, as they both look like blobs in blankets to me.

"Will you hold Daisy?" My sister indicates her head towards Daisy lying in her little bed.

Without thought, I wash my hands in the sink then pick up my niece. She makes faint noises as I get her settled in my arms and sit down. She peers up at me, but I remember someone mentioned they can't really see far.

"Wow, these kiddos are growing fast," I remark as I stare at Daisy.

"Yeah, I know. Tomorrow, I'll take them home, and that'll be exhausting but good to be home."

"We can get you help, just say the word," I remind her, looking up from Daisy.

"I know. Mom is going to help me the first few weeks, and Steve will be back on leave this weekend, so let's see. Maybe it's a better idea if Mason comes back home earlier, and maybe Sadie would be willing to come to my place to care for Mason," my sister suggests.

"Oh."

"Is there a problem?"

"I just… I don't know. I mean, your house is a little farther out, and I just assumed Mason would stay with me while you and Steve have some time to yourselves." It's genuine, but Mason back at my sister's sooner also means that I see less of Sadie.

"Sadie is really sweet. She texts me photos and updates all the time. I actually feel like I've gotten to know her a little," my sister mentions, and this piques my interest.

"Oh yeah? About Mason, you mean?" I focus on the baby in my arms even though I feel my sister's gaze on me.

"Yes, Mason. Should there be other updates?" she raises.

I look up, and lo and behold, my sister is giving me the authoritarian look.

"Nope. No other updates," I reply blankly.

"Liar."

That twin superpower really can be a conversation killer sometimes.

"She said something?" I'm surprised.

"No, but your face right now says enough, so spill it."

I sigh and debate how honest to be. "It's nothing, okay. We just talk a lot."

My sister puts Lily back in her bed. "And?"

I roll my head, knowing there's no escape. "And we enjoy one another's company."

"My theory is correct." My sister sits back on her bed.

"Don't stress about it, okay? Mason is happy as a clam."

She puts a hand on her hip as she sits. "And my brother is happy as a clam too?"

Just then Mason comes running in straight to Zoe for a hug. Sadie is following in tow, and she looks absolutely radiant today. Her hair is down and in thick waves. Her blue dress has a few buttons that I could rip off, and her eyes flutter my way, but she quickly focuses on my sister.

"Can I hold one?" Mason asks. Zoe nods and brings Lily to him.

It's all in the background to me, as I'm entranced by

Sadie. The movements in my arms bring me back to the fact that I'm holding a baby.

"Crap, I think she's about to do something," I note aloud.

"Oh, probably needs to be burped. Just wait while I get Mason set up. Or maybe, Sadie, you know how?" my sister asks.

"You mean burp a baby? I, uhm… I think so." Sadie looks at Daisy, unsure, then my sister.

"Please? You can hold her," my sister reassures Sadie that she doesn't mind.

Sadie offers me a half-smile as she takes the baby from my arms, and my eyes never leave her.

For the next two minutes, I am mesmerized by watching Sadie hold and cradle a baby. It's sending an array of mixed messages to my brain. Slightly worried, slightly admiring, not complaining about the view…

"When do I get to come home?" Mason asks, and all the adults look at one another.

"Aren't you having fun with Uncle Logan?" My sister seems to be working some reverse psychology to avoid an answer.

"Of course he is, and we're going away for a few days to go fishing," I remind everyone.

"Rumble comes too?" Mason asks.

Sadie and I look at one another as we both slightly cringe at the reminder.

"I'm not sure he would like the traveling, but I'll check on him while you're away," Sadie answers.

My sister's head perks up toward Sadie. "You're not going with?"

"Well, I don't think I'll be needed. I mean, it's uncle and nephew time." Sadie focuses on Daisy in her arms, cooing slightly.

Zoe looks between Sadie and me. Already I know there's a wheel turning in her head.

"Oh? But Logan always ends up having work calls or checking e-mails. What will he do if Mason is around?"

"I suppose that's possible," Sadie notes but is too occupied with the baby.

"I would feel better if you go along, Sadie. I know being around them both full-time is a lot, but then I know Mason is eating something other than ice cream and actually going to sleep at a normal time. Plus, Logan could use a break too. Please, Sadie? It'll make me feel better," my sister pleads and lays out her reasons.

The entire time, I study my sister. My eyes narrow, and I know this is my sister's way of convincing Sadie to come with me. It's surprising, as I thought she wouldn't be on board. But my sister is very much on the bandwagon it seems. I know for a fact she doesn't care about me going away alone with Mason. She let me take Mason to Disneyland in California last year. A wry smile forms on my face at this unexpected cheerleader from the sidelines.

"What you're saying makes sense," I confirm then turn my gaze to Sadie.

"I guess, well, I mean… okay. I'll come on this little getaway."

She most definitely will be coming…

21

LOGAN

Friday morning, Mason and I picked Sadie up on our way out of the city. We use my Range Rover since my Aston Martin wouldn't fit all of us and luggage. A shame, as it would have been perfect for cruising up along the lake today with Sadie's hair blowing in the wind, but the SUV life isn't too bad. Mason is in his own world in the back seat, looking at his tablet, and Sadie sits in the front admiring the views. It's a perfect summer day with blue skies and clear views over the lake. Traffic is a breeze, so it's a smooth ride.

"This is your music choice?" I have to double-check because I let her pick the music while I'm driving.

She turns her head to me with a defensive look. "Yes. Do you have a problem?"

"Never took you for a country fan," I remark.

"A little Hunter Hayes and Sam Hunt make my day every day." She sounds rather chirpy.

"Fair enough. Did you listen to the playlist I sent you when I discovered what you named me on your phone?" I have to remind her with a smile to myself.

She shakes her head silently to herself. "I did, actually, and your tastes aren't bad. A lot of indie happening. I like it."

"I have good taste," I remind her with a smirk.

She looks over her shoulder to double-check Mason is in his own world, and he is.

"We should be there in about ten minutes. No clue what the place is like since I had Jen book everything."

"I'm sure she has a good sense of booking what you like, since she does it so often for you."

"We made good time. Four hours and twenty minutes." I'm proud of myself.

Sadie gives me a side glare. I see it in the corner of my eye. "You weren't exactly abiding by the speed limits, but yeah, you got us here in no time. I should probably look into an option for lunch; Mason will be hangry soon." Sadie pulls out her phone and begins to swipe.

I reach out to prevent her from searching. "Stop it. You're not on duty, you're here because I…" I stop when I realize I'm about to say because I want her here and not as the nanny.

She looks up at me with what I could swear is a hopeful glance.

"I mean, we'll figure it out. There's the diner I went to as a kid; I'm kind of hoping that's still around."

"Right."

It's a little stiff in the air for the remaining two minutes in the car, but the moment we arrive at the rental house, I know I owe Jen big time. Maybe even a paid vacation for her.

I hear an audible, "Whoa," from the backseat, and in the front seat, Sadie has a beaming look that in return makes me smile.

I park the car in front of the picture-perfect house along the lake, complete with a boat dock, deck, and outside sitting area. There's a fire pit, and I can't help noticing the jacuzzi. *Great choice, Jen.*

We all hop out of the car and walk toward the front door.

Romantic fire—check. Jacuzzi with a bikini-covered Sadie—check. I should probably wonder why I want a romantic night with her so badly. Not a night of fantastic sex —we're good at that. No, I want to hold her as we open a bottle of Merlot and talk.

My nephew running ahead knocks me back into reality. "Hey. Don't run or play near the water unless Sadie or I are there," I call out and warn him with a stern tone that I don't exactly enjoy. I want to be the cool uncle.

He runs back to us, and we all head inside, taking in our not-so-humble abode for the coming weekend. Mason runs upstairs to check out the rooms, and my eyes stay fixated on Sadie who smiles at the box waiting for her on the counter in the kitchen.

She peers up to me, and she toys with the red string on the white box. "What's this?"

"I don't know," I pretend as I lean over the counter across from her.

She gives me a look that says she isn't quite convinced. Opening the box, her smile grows wide. "You remembered?" She sounds surprised.

"We couldn't stay at that bed-and-breakfast you mentioned thanks to my nephew. Did you know some bed-and-breakfasts have a great policy of no kids? But I thought you would still want those specialty cookies with cherries you read about."

She walks to me and steps into my arms that I wrap around her to pull her tightly against me. "That's really sweet." She kisses my cheek.

A chaste cheek kiss just doesn't fly.

I quickly dive down and in to capture her mouth in a hard, greedy kiss. She likes it, I know because she makes that noise that drives me wild. But she also pushes me away.

"You're going to get us in trouble," she teases.

"I like trouble with you."

We both enjoy our banter for a second more before breaking away when we hear Mason charging down the stairs.

"Can we go out on the lake?" he asks.

I ruffle his hair with my hand. "Sure. But let's go get some ice cream and fresh bait for fishing."

Mason's face lights up like a Christmas tree.

———

THE REST of the afternoon is relaxing. We had to wait outside this classic ice cream parlor that makes great sundaes because of all the tourists. As we waited in line, my eyes were glued on Sadie who was in shorts and a white shirt today, her hair down and shiny. Watching her interact with Mason as they picked out which ice cream flavor to go for was just, well… adorable.

Then after getting a few supplies from the quaint little lakeside town, we headed back to the house, first stopping by a lighthouse for some photos. Now I have a bunch of pics on my phone of my nephew, Sadie, and picture-perfect views of the lake. Not that I'm a competitive guy, but our photos gave the family from Minnesota next to us a run for their money. We nailed the funny photos, the obligatory family photos, and the quick shots of Sadie—the camera didn't do her justice.

Sadie wanted to give Mason and me some time alone while we went to a nearby spot for fishing, and Sadie stayed at the house to read and soak in some sun.

We're standing out on a nearby dock. "Alright, hold on, we got him," I tell Mason as I help him reel in the line of his fishing rod. We've caught a few mid-sized trout. The fish wobbles on the hook before I take the pole from Mason and manage to get the fish in the bucket on the deck.

"Do you think I'll do this with my new dad?"

I look at Mason, and in all honesty, I wasn't anticipating this unexpected serious conversation. But since I'm a pro at staying neutral, I persevere—especially since Steve is not only fairly new to my sister, but he is sure as hell new to Mason. Although a good guy, it's still too early for me to commit to team Steve.

"You mean Steve?" I look at him, double-checking, and Mason nods. "Well, I'm sure he'll take you fishing when he can. But it doesn't matter, you have me, okay?" I rub his shoulder.

"Will he move in with us?"

"You mean with your mom and sisters? Yeah, but you know he won't be home much, right? His job isn't like mine. He doesn't go to an office," I remind him.

"I know, but maybe he'll make my mom happy the way you make Sadie happy."

Whoa, the kid throws a plot twist at me.

I laugh under my breath to myself, slightly nervous. "What makes you say that, buddy?"

Mason looks up at me. "Because she always seems happy when it's close to dinner time and when you come home from work. Just like you smile a lot when she's around. You even come back early from work."

"It's to see you too."

"I know, and I like that we're reading a lot together—"

"Your reading is great. We even finished that book about that dog who's a captain in three days."

He shrugs a shoulder. "I know, but you kiss Sadie. It's gross, but that must mean you like her."

My eyes go wide, and just like that, the kid has managed to make a grown man freeze. I play it cool. "So, you saw that, did you?"

"You always kiss her when you think I'm not looking. Are you going to marry her?"

I could really use an interruption right now. I even glance around to see if there's a chance for that miracle, but there's nothing but blue skies, birds flying, and the sound of the occasional boat passing by. *Damn it, Wisconsin.*

"Mason, when you're an adult, you can be together and not get married. Sometimes you need to get to know one another and that can take a long time, even years." I'm trying to think of how to phrase this whole situation.

We gather our fishing supplies. "Hmm. So, you'll be with Sadie for years?"

Crap. Now I've confused the kid.

We walk toward the car. "How about we go biking tomorrow?" Changing topics tends to work with Mason.

"Could we?" He sounds excited as he runs toward the car.

Thank fuck for children's short attention spans.

———

WHEN WE RETURN around dinner time, Sadie is busy preparing things in various bowls. We arrive in the kitchen, and Mason holds up his bucket with pride.

"Did you bring us dinner? I only made the sides, so I was counting on your amazing fishing skills." Sadie smiles at Mason and leans down to check out the bucket.

"We did. I got three fish," Mason says proudly.

"Wow!" Sadie glances up at me with a puzzled look. "Am I expected to cook those?"

"Is that not in your cooking skills?" I ask with fake seriousness. Her face goes slightly concerned. "Relax, I can do it," I assure her.

"You cook fish? As in prepare the fish and cook it?" Now her look is skeptical.

I take the bucket from my nephew. "I do. A skill you didn't know I have." Our eyes hold for a second, and she has a wry smile on her face.

"Really?" She's still not convinced.

"Yes. I just never have time to cook," I admit and begin to head outside where there's a grill. If we're going to cook fish, then we will cook it right.

Thirty minutes later, Sadie is pouring me a glass of white wine as Mason plays in the grass with his soccer ball.

"Okay, so I now know you fish and cook. Any other hidden talents?" Sadie settles into her chair next to the table outside. The sun is beginning to set, making her look extra magical this evening.

"Now, now, Sadie, I think you know when you say that you're challenging me."

She chortles before sighing. "I think we'll have to eat inside; the mosquitoes up here are out like crazy at night."

"Way worse than the city. Hope this doesn't put a damper on our Jacuzzi plans." I'm now deeply concerned.

"We had plans?" she says, teasing me.

"Yes. It's been a while since I haven't checked e-mails and just relaxed. I plan on enjoying all the perks of being on vacation," I remark as I serve the fish onto plates.

"You really are doing a mini-vacation, off the grid?"

"I am," I answer proudly.

"Wow. Why the change?" She stands to help me with the plates.

I have to think for a second, but it doesn't take long. "It just feels right in this moment."

She smiles gently at me, with the corners of her mouth tugging, and I'm not sure who enjoys my words more—me or her.

After eating dinner, reading with Mason, and getting the kiddo to bed, I come down the stairs to look for Sadie. She isn't in the kitchen. When I look outside, I see in silhouette the subtle swinging of the hammock and assume that's where she is. The moment I open the sliding door, I hear the sound of crickets from the woods behind the side of the house and the occasional seagull from the lakeside. Walking over to the hammock, I instantly see Sadie lying with her eyes staring up toward the sky.

"You can handle the mosquitos, but no Jacuzzi?" I fake disappointment as I slide onto the hammock to lie with her.

She adjusts her body to make room for me.

"Nah, I wanted to look at the stars. Mason asleep?" she asks, her eyes never leaving the sky.

I peer up to the dark night too, our shoulders touching. "Out like a light." For a second, I soak in the view, the sounds, and the feeling of her so close. Without thought, I let my fingers walk along the soft skin of her arm, encouraging her hand to open for me, and it does. We interlink our fingers. "I forgot the sky is so much clearer up here."

"It is. A few extra shooting stars, plus the occasional lightning bug. It's peaceful."

Interlaced hands aren't enough, I need her closer. My arm swoops up and around her to pull her to me. She quickly remolds herself into me, and Sadie almost shivers.

"Are you cold?"

"A little. It cools off quite a bit during the night," she mentions, so I begin to rub heat into her arms, which only makes her almost purr as she nestles into me. "You think you'll take Mason here again? Make it a tradition?"

"Why not? It's a quick ride up from Chicago, and he seems to enjoy it here." I think about the way I used to come here with my grandfather until I hit my teenage years, when I felt hanging with my friends was more important. Then I think about the summers of the future as my nephew grows older. It'll be just me and him; Sadie won't be there to wait for us and keep us in line.

For the first time in a long time, I think about me a year from now and so on. That's not like me, not when women are involved. I definitely wouldn't normally feel a dull pain in my chest at the idea of a particular woman being absent from my life.

But for once I do.

"One day I hope to bring my kids here," she says, and that dull pain turns sharp. I'm reminded why I can't have her in my future—she wants it all. I'm not that kind of guy.

"They'll like that," I manage to gulp out.

We lie there as the hammock sways gently, and my thoughts run rampant.

I don't care if I'm the right guy for her or not.

In this moment. In this weekend. She is mine, and I'm hers.

We don't need to think past the present, which is exactly

why the words flow out of my mouth. "I want you in my bed, Sadie, to sleep after I take my time with you. I want to fall asleep with you in my arms, and when I wake, I want you to still be in my arms," I declare to her, and as much as it surprises me, the conviction I have in my voice, it's only the truth.

Her hand splays across my chest as she moves to her side to look down at me. "Logan, I don't think that's a good idea. Mason could—"

"I'll take the chance. Call me selfish, but I know what I need, and I need you in my bed." My tone is quite direct and sharp, but so help me, I'm a man desperately wanting her. The feeling of her silky hair, her smell like flowers, and her body that I belong in.

She must pick up on the pleading in my words. "Okay," she replies as her hand caresses my cheek. "Okay, Logan."

I smirk to myself before my mouth covers hers for a hard, possessive kiss, immediately causing her to murmur.

Sadie swings her legs off the hammock and stands. She holds a hand out to me, inviting me to follow her. The moment my fingers reconnect with the skin of her hand, I warm.

Our journey back inside, through the house and up the stairs, is a peaceful journey. Slow and silent, a different type of anticipation building between us. I tug her arm toward me to stop her when we reach my bedroom door, and I kiss the top of her hair, as her back is to my front.

"You're on the pill, right?" I ask softly. Normally, I always use condoms, but I have no control with her. I need her to really be mine.

"Yes… I want that too," she replies gently, as our minds are aligned, yet I hear the excitement in her voice before she places her hand on the doorknob and opens the door.

The lights are off, but the curtains are open to let in the moonlight through the balcony doors that wrap around the corner room.

I close the door behind us, and, immediately, I turn her around by placing my hands firmly on her hips.

Our eyes meet in the moonlight, in a daze, her lips parted and her breath heavy. I begin to work the buttons of her shorts then pull them down without our gaze breaking. My long fingers skirt the edges of her panties, toying and hooking under the rim, tracing the outline. Her little gasp reminds me she is always affected by my touch.

She grabs and scrunches the fabric of my t-shirt and peels it up and over my head.

"Come here," I whisper. I have a firm grip on her obliques and pull her flush to me.

Our lips meet for a kiss where my tongue ventures out to find her own. My hands cup her face to kiss her, as if this kiss is poignant and may go down in history as the confirmation that she has me thinking of another future. Pulling away, I kiss her forehead.

She touches my arms and encourages me to move to the edge of the bed. I sit on the mattress, and it dips beneath me as she steps between my knees. I'm in a perfect position for watching her take her shirt off, and as she's about to reach for her bra clasp, I stop her. Instead, I reach up to undo the clasp for her, feeling the goosebumps from her shiver as her bra falls to the floor.

Sadie places a knee on each side of my hips on the bed, coming to sit on top of my hard cock. I want her hands, her mouth, her pussy—anything she'll give me. The mesh of her panties is driving me insane as I feel the damp heat. My face dives between her pert breasts, my teeth gently grazing her skin, and her head falls back, her hair falling everywhere. My mouth glides along her milky skin to a hard nipple that I take in my mouth. I suck, and instantly it causes her to move her pussy on top of me in a rolling movement.

Her soft moan encourages me, the sound sending a signal to my cock that we're heading toward a path to release.

She pushes me back on the bed, placing her hands across my chest and leaning over me. The moonlight allows me to see her eyes gazing down on me as her tongue licks her lip. Truly, she is the most beautiful woman I've seen.

I scoop up her hands and we interlace our fingers, causing her to move a few inches forward as I place our hands against the mattress on both sides. We take a few moments to look at one another, and I grin as I lean my head up to meet hers for a playful searing kiss where I can feel her smile against my teeth. She's happy, and I like that, I like that a lot.

Hooking a leg around her legs, I roll us, so she's lying on her back on the bed under me—the way she's supposed to be tonight.

Again, we look at one another. It's affection, I'm not that blind.

Dragging my lips along the corners of her mouth to her cheek, I reach her ear and nuzzle. "Sadie, I'm going to take you so deep and not let you go. You'll never forget this."

Her breath catches, but she nods with her head resting on the pillow.

"Please touch me," she begs so innocently.

"Show me. Show me exactly what you want," I request.

I love the feeling of my hand being dragged together with hers along our bodies until it arrives between her thighs. It's the path I was hoping she would choose.

"Feel what you do to me," she rasps, with her mouth reaching up trying to capture another kiss.

Together we claw the edges of her panties and pull

them down in a swift movement before she guides my fingers to the destination she wants. Sliding along her slit is exactly what turns me harder, pressure swirling to my groin.

The smell of her sweet arousal sets off chemicals in me, I want to take her. Her honey is drowning my fingers.

Finding her clit, I gently swirl and rub against her. Her subtle moans grow louder with each stroke.

"You're going to feel so good inside me," she moans, and I couldn't agree more.

Her body curves into me, and her hand becomes limp from all her energy intensifying around her clit.

"You want me inside you, baby?" I speak against the skin of her neck.

"God yes, please, Logan. I'm ready for you, I want this." Damn right she is.

I remove my briefs, and my cock is relieved to finally be free. Taking her hand, I bring it to my cock. "This is what you do to me."

She breathes heavily and moans as she pumps a few strokes. Her knee moves over me, as if she's trying to ride the air to get us closer.

As I move to capture her under me, her legs part open.

The head of my cock slides up and down between her folds to tease us both. I'm getting soaked from her silk. She is so damn wet that I slip right into her, making her gasp in surprise.

"Feel that, Sadie?" I groan as I move deeper into her.

"Yes," she says huskily.

"This is how you should always be fucked, feeling your sweet pussy as it wraps around my big cock." I move in a rhythm, going delirious from the wetness and warmth surrounding my length.

My hand holds her neck firmly in place, since I'm not letting her look anywhere else but into my eyes.

Completely lost, with our eyes locked and her body meeting me on every thrust, my heart rate shoots up, and I'm not entirely sure it's because of the sex… or if it's her. Truthfully, I know the answer.

Deep. That's what I need, and I fill her until there is nowhere else to go.

"Logan," she cries. My mouth instantly meets hers—we can't be too loud.

"Ride the wave with me," I encourage her. I feel her getting close, and I'm about to burst.

Her orgasm grips her as she pants my name as quietly as possible against my mouth. Trembling around my cock, her body convulses.

"I'm there with you," I tell her.

I'm tumbling with her down the same path. I release, I jerk, I still.

I lie there, inside her. Sadie holding me. Sadie kissing my hair tenderly.

"Just stay in me, don't leave," she gently requests. "I don't want to forget this feeling." Her words sound like she's reminiscing or that she knows this won't be forever. It tugs me somewhere inside too.

I can't think about that now. I kiss her on the mouth and not gently.

My arms move around her head to keep her caged in and to support my weight.

"I don't care if I go to hell, I literally just felt heaven."

It makes her laugh quietly. "That's such a line," she teases me.

I kiss down her neck as I mutter against her skin, "But a hundred percent true."

I hear her sigh as her nails brush up and down my back.

Giving her a quick peck, I reluctantly pull out, and already I miss it. Heading to the bathroom off the room, I grab a towel and return to bed where Sadie looks completely relaxed. I pass her the towel.

"Hmm. Not sure I need it. I think I want to feel you running down my thigh all night."

It makes me grin. This. Woman. Is. A. Gift.

"Good answer," I reply as I grab my boxer briefs to pull back on.

"But can I have a shirt? I can't lie in here naked just in case your nephew surprises us—which is also an issue, by the way—and you have made me kind of lifeless so I can't walk to my room for my pajamas," she explains, lying there like a jellyfish.

I growl. "Solid point, but it's not how I would prefer for you to be in my bed."

Grabbing a t-shirt from my bag, I toss it in her direction, but then quickly slide into bed and stop her from putting it on.

"Let me stare at you naked for a little bit."

I eye her from head to toe as my fingertips explore her skin in lines, admiring her completely naked, her nipples stiffening from the coolness.

"You've seen me naked, and it's cold, so request denied." She smirks before putting my shirt on.

"Fine. But you in my shirt is also a good view." I fold her into my embrace, and she kisses my chest.

"Not complaining."

Nor am I.

23

SADIE

Last night felt like a dream. It wasn't just sex; it was an intense feeling—an overwhelming feeling. We were as close as we have been, and we were so with intention.

Sleeping in his arms, I never flinched or moved during the night. I was in a deep sleep until early morning when I woke to find Logan ready to go. It's a good thing I woke up prepared for him, because not even a few blinks from my eyes, and he slid into me. We made it quick yet sensual, on our sides with my leg hooked over his, his hands cradling my face as we moved together in sync. The sunrise highlighted his muscles and his piercing eyes. We were silent, as the crack of a smile said enough.

I'm getting in too deep. He must feel that too?

The sizzling of the griddle on the stove brings me back to the present. Logan went for a run while I showered, quickly changed, and came downstairs to make breakfast. Right on cue, Mason arrives downstairs in his pajamas as I pour pancake mix onto the griddle.

"Hey, Mase, did you sleep okay?" I move the pancakes around the heat.

"Can we have chocolate chips in the pancakes?"

"Mmm, I don't think we have those. But I'm sure later today you'll go for ice cream again."

"But I want chocolate chips." His temper woke up on the wrong side of the bed this morning, clearly.

Just as I hear the sliding door open, I tell Mason, "Well, I said no, and I'm sure the pancake syrup will make the pancakes sweet enough. We even have strawberries."

"What's going on?" Logan asks as he opens the fridge and grabs a bottle of water.

"Mason is adamant he has chocolate chips in his pancakes," I say through a grinding smile.

Logan gives Mason a stern look. "If Sadie says no then it's no."

Mason pouts. "That's unfair. You're just siding with her because you kiss her."

Logan nearly chokes on his water, and my face turns puzzled as my adrenaline spikes. Mason heads to the television area in a huff, but I know he'll be okay. Instead, I slowly turn my gaze to Logan.

"I think I forgot to mention something to you," he notes.

"Uh, yes. Fill me in and quick," I urge.

Logan circles his head, rubbing his neck. "It seems the kid is pretty smart and already figured out that, well, you and I are fans of one another. He told me yesterday during fishing."

My face drops and I panic. "What?! You're only now telling me?" I whisper loudly, but I don't think Mason can hear. I turn the griddle off and aggressively dish out the pancakes onto plates.

"Hey, he doesn't seem too bothered." Logan touches my arm, but I jerk it away.

"That's good, but I don't know. Should I feel weird about this?" I hear the question in my voice.

"Nah."

"Logan, we're only going to confuse him, and your sis—"

"I think knows too." He says it so simply.

My face goes blank, and he looks at me almost amused. He even has the audacity to grab a pancake and take a bite without letting his gaze leave me.

"So, she… doesn't care?" I stagger out, trying to figure out these new facts.

"Now that my nieces are born, she seems pretty peachy. Steve is back too. I don't think she'll be putting me in the doghouse now for sleeping with the very hot nanny." He gives me a devilish grin that is sinfully sexy.

These are all good updates except… they aren't.

It just means the inevitable will come sooner. That doesn't bode well for me. At some point soon, I will no longer be the secret thrill for Logan, and life will return to normal when Mason goes back to his mom. This news is all a reminder that while before I could say we shouldn't sleep together so we didn't upset his sister, that's no longer the case. Now it's apparent that our remaining issue is that Logan doesn't do relationships. *That's* our issue.

Something is bothering me, and I can't pinpoint what exactly. I always knew that Mason and Zoe finding out were a possibility. But now that they know, they're probably wondering what Logan and I are to one another, and that's what causes me to feel empty in my stomach. I want an answer too.

Internally, I make a promise to myself to address the bigger picture—the fact that the demise of our relationship is approaching.

But not until after the weekend.

For now, I decide to brush my reservations to the side.

Logan looks over my shoulder toward the background of cartoons and seems to have the green light before kissing my forehead.

"Now that's all clear, let's have a good rest of the weekend," he assures me.

I attempt a smile, but it's weakened.

THE REST OF THE MORNING, Logan and Mason went biking. I wanted them to have man-to-man time because I feel Mason could use it, especially since I think Logan fills in on the father-figure aspect of Mason's life. I met them after their ride outside a little diner that is a throwback to the fifties.

"I have a great idea for after lunch." Logan grins as he pours ketchup onto his fries.

"Oh yeah?" I ask as I show Mason his chicken fingers and move his shake away. I'm sitting next to him in the booth.

"There's a beautiful bluff nearby that we can walk to," Logan explains, and he is beaming and seems very excited.

"Sounds good," I answer before biting into my BLT sandwich.

The sound of his phone going off interrupts us, and he excuses himself for a minute.

"Having fun, Mason?" I ask.

"Yeah. It'll suck when I have to go live with the babies. They'll just cry all the time."

I nudge Mason gently with my arm. "We don't say suck, and you'll love it. You're the big brother. Remember how you told me that? Plus, babies do a lot of funny things that that you'll love."

"Like what?"

"Uhm… they burp, they laugh at silly faces, they grow super-fast. One day soon, they'll always want to play with you." I nibble on a few fries.

"I guess. Do you think Steve will be like Uncle Logan?" Mason looks almost sullen.

I touch his arm attentively and turn him gently in my direction. "Is that what really worries you?"

"He'll only have time for his kids and my mom."

"Hey, I haven't met him, but I don't think he looks at your sisters and you differently. It's all new for him too. Sometimes we just need to give people a chance." I'm doing my best to give Mason a pep talk, but I quickly scan the room, waiting for Logan to return.

"Can I come live with you and Uncle Logan?"

I laugh nervously. "Well, I don't live with your uncle. I'm only there when you're there."

"But maybe after you both get to know each other, then you'll live there. That's what Uncle Logan said," Mason explains before attacking a chicken finger.

I don't know what to say. The clearing of a throat interrupts my blank thought.

"He means I said sometimes grown-ups can spend time together to get to know one another. Not everyone needs to be married," Logan explains as he slides back into the booth.

Right. *Of course.*

I nod and again choose to move us all quickly on. "Everything okay?"

Logan's lips purse, and I can tell there's something, but he doesn't want to discuss it in front of Mason. I don't think it has to do with me, rather the call he had.

Under the table my foot reaches for his calf of pure toned muscle. My toe digs into his flesh, and it makes him smile to himself and give me a wink. Whatever was bothering him must be gone, since my move puts him back in better spirits.

After lunch, we make our way to the bluff over the lake. It's quite secluded, and although it's Lake Michigan, you feel like you're almost in the Caribbean with clear blue water.

As I sit on a rock with Logan's and Mason's clothes at my feet, I watch the scene in front of me with the afternoon sun hitting me. You couldn't ask for a more beautiful summer day.

"Isn't it really cold?" I ask as Mason walks into the water, oblivious to the temperature.

He shakes his head at me. "Are you going to jump off the rocks, Uncle Logan?"

Logan is busy pulling his shirt up and off. "Of course, want to join me?"

"Absolutely not, he's too small," I say in a hushed tone to Logan.

"Relax, Sadie, I won't let him go alone," Logan promises as he throws his shirt to my feet.

"It's really high," Mason comments.

"It's not that high, and you should do things that you've never done before. Do things that may scare you, because you sometimes need to conquer your fears. It might be the best thing to happen to you," Logan encourages.

Mason looks at his uncle with curiosity. "Did you jump when you were my age?"

Logan touches his nephew's shoulder. "I did, but it took my grandfather to convince me. You can also sit with Sadie, but I'm going to jump."

"It does look cool," Mason says in awe. Logan heads up the rocks with Mason in tow.

Although they're quite a bit ahead of me, I can hear enough, especially as it's quiet around us.

"Are you sure you want to do this?" Logan checks with Mason, and he nods.

"Okay. Take my hand." Logan warmly offers his hand to his nephew with a soft smile.

It's in that moment when they jump hand in hand that my heart tightens from the feeling that I have never truly experienced until now. I can no longer say it's fun or lust. Watching Logan swimming with Mason on his back, I know what I've been feeling all weekend.

I have completely fallen for Logan Jax.

My heart is his… but he doesn't want it. Because Logan Jax doesn't fall in love.

24

SADIE

Leaning against the balcony, I look out at the dark sky over the lake. Sometimes I admire how a clear night has the ability to calm me so easily. Sighing, I know what I need to do. Right now, however, I'm going to pretend nothing has changed so I can selfishly enjoy more moments with Logan.

The cascading of arms around me over my satin robe makes the lines of a smile form on my face as Logan pulls me flush against him.

"Mason's asleep?"

"Mmhmm," he mumbles, bunching my hair up and dragging his lips slowly along the back of my neck, and in the process, my whole body tingles from the feeling.

"Logan," I purr a warning, but his other hand is already sliding up my thigh, and his fingers tug on the hem of my panties.

"Let me take you right here, under the stars. We'll be quick," he murmurs into my ear. He's already moving down the lace and releases my hair.

I feel my channel pulsing, and a release of arousal coming

out of me as I bite my lip and press my ass against him. "Logan," I rasp.

"Bend forward, Sadie," he whispers. He encourages me with his fingertips gently pressing into my back, causing me to use the railing for support.

He stops, and there's a silent pause that makes me wonder what he's doing. I glance over my shoulder as I feel his hand rubbing a circle on my ass. He's admiring the view, and it makes me anxious when I notice he's studying me.

"What are you wearing?" he asks, his lips pursing out into a near hiss.

"Oh, uhm, just something I had in my bag," I play innocent and look away from him.

In a swift move, he unties my robe and opens it. His eyes roam me up and down to assess his prize. Leaving the robe open, he leans down and moves the fabric of my satin tank top, so my nipples are out and erect. The cool air hits my skin, but not for long. His mouth licks one of my nipples while he peers up at me to watch me as I moan. His other arm wraps around to pull me against him to feel his hard cock.

Letting the nipple go, he plays with my other nipple using his fingers and continues as he speaks. "I'm taking you right here and now. Now bend the fuck over because I need to be inside you." He slams his mouth onto mine to show me how serious he is, before he quickly spins me around, and I find myself in a ninety-degree angle against the railing.

The sound of him unzipping his jeans thrills me, and the moment his cock slides into me, I close my eyes. The strong pumps make my tits jiggle on every deep stroke. My open robe hangs off my body as Logan thrusts into me with purpose.

"I can't get enough of you," he grits out.

"Oh my God," I pant as his movements quicken.

When we finally reach our end, he holds me as we lean forward to the railing, breathless.

I've never done something so intimate out in the public, although nobody could see, but that's just Logan. He has the ability to make me be comfortable with anything, as long as he's involved.

He kisses my shoulder softly before adjusting my robe on my body, then he offers his hand to me to walk back inside together.

We fall into bed and lie there looking at one another, neither of us ready to sleep. A type of silence overtakes us, and I can tell he's thinking, and so am I. But I know we're not contemplating the same thought.

He lies on this side to look at me as his finger reaches between my legs to confirm he left his mark. Just the touch turns me on yet again, but his eyes tell me that he's too lost in thought.

"A penny for your thoughts?" I ask as he wipes his fingers on my stomach then across my breasts.

"Nothing. Just relaxing in this moment."

"You seem a little off since that phone call." I wonder if that's where his mind is.

"It was Zoe. She wants Mason to come back to her place after the weekend, earlier than planned. Steve got extended leave, so they feel like they need more time to bond together as a family, which makes sense…"

The corner of my mouth curves up. "But then no more Mason at your house and maybe you'll miss that."

He shrugs. "No. I mean, at least then I can get back to my normal life." He brushes the topic under the rug and acts like he isn't affected, but I can see he is.

"We both can. I guess you're not my boss anymore…"

His eyes shoot to me and turn almost… well, I can't

pinpoint it. Possessive or stormy. I don't know, but he kisses me with force, as if he needs to remind me of something. Something I may never know.

Pulling away, I push him to his back and move to cuddle against his chest with my leg propped over his waist, with the beating of his heart thumping against my cheek.

He combs my hair with his fingers and kisses my head. I wonder if he's this way with every woman he sleeps with or is it just me? Tender and sweet. I want to be special, but I won't ask him to change. That's not who he is.

I kiss his chest before gently closing my eyes and soaking in this moment, knowing I'm going to need to rip this band-aid off when get back to the city.

———

"WANT to go grab a bite to eat before I get you in the shower?" Logan asks with that suave grin as he opens the door to his home.

Staring at Logan, I plant my feet firmly in the hallway between the elevator and his front door. We just dropped Mason off at Zoe's after our weekend away, and I know the time has come.

"No, Logan, I think…" I hear the dryness of my throat and internally remind myself to remain strong. "Logan, the thing is… well. I'm not going to set myself up for a big fall."

Seriousness washes over his face, and he takes a step in my direction but stops.

"I told you once I would try fun, and maybe we are just fun—"

He grabs my hand. "Sadie, you're more than just fun."

My eyes shoot up to him. I bite my bottom lip. "So, what? We have dinner here, sleep together, talk, and then one day…"

I stop, and I could swear I see pain in his face. "In the long run, we don't want the same. I'm not going to let myself invest time and emotion into something that will never be what I want it to be. I'm setting myself up for heartache if we continue like this, because eventually, we will reach a cross-roads. I'm smart—too smart. A lot of women think they can change the guy who can't be tamed, but I'm not even going to try. Because what you want shouldn't be forced."

"How do you know what I want?" He studies me.

I shake my head slightly. "You've made it clear repeatedly that you never want to get re-married or have kids. You don't want to settle down with anyone, and that's something I want one day… with someone. If we keep doing this then I may miss my opportunity to meet someone who wants a lifetime with me."

His nostrils flare slightly, and he adjusts his neck out of discomfort. "Sadie," he nearly growls and closes our distance, with his hand reaching to cradle my face.

"Listen to me, I know my limits, Logan. I already know I've crossed the line of being in too deep." My bottom lip quivers, and I feel a sting of tears in my eyes. "You are that perfect investment to me, but I wouldn't get any return on that investment since we both know what you want in your future." I give him the weakest half-smile of my life since I referenced his work in conjunction with my heart.

He rubs his thumb against my lips before kissing my forehead.

"Bye, Logan."

He grabs my wrist to prevent me from leaving, but then reluctantly lets me go.

———

Curled up on the sofa in my brother's apartment, I feel numb. It's only been one day and already I miss Logan. I repeatedly tell myself it was the right thing to do, yet I secretly hope he'll come barging through the door, shaking me and telling me I was wrong. But he won't, and my heart will thank me one day.

It's a thought reiterated by Ruby and Emily's text messages confirming I did the right thing.

The sound of the front door opening makes me sigh. As much as I wish it would be someone else, it's my brother Wes who is in town for a few days. I throw the blanket off me and swing my legs off the couch. My attempt to get off the couch fails. I feel like a zombie—and possibly look like one too.

Looking up, I see my brother carrying a perfectly wrapped fruit basket, and that makes me hop off the couch.

"This arrived for you." Wes hands me the basket that I accept in wonder.

"Thanks," I say, studying the basket.

"Does this have something to do with the asshole you got involved with?" Wes isn't afraid to speak his mind. He must've somehow convinced Emily to spill the beans, which would be slightly odd since they don't particularly speak, but I wouldn't put it past him.

I didn't tell him anything about me and Logan, but since my brother has played the field, then I can only imagine he's guessed. I give him a daggered stare in response.

Sliding a few steps back, I place the basket on the coffee table and search for the card. I find the cream-colored envelope with my name.

Pulling the paper out, I read the card, and immediately my heart aches, cracks, then crashes. My lips tremble as I feel the burn of a cry creeping up my throat.

Sadie,
Thank you for all your help this summer.
Best of luck,
L. Jax

Message received. Now, I just need to move on.

Arriving home, I sigh, throwing my tie to the kitchen counter. It's eleven pm, and I head to the fridge, hoping I still have a bottle of specialty beer.

Opening the fridge, I see a bottle along with a carton of eggs. Nothing else in there, not like a week ago. A week ago, it was filled with vegetables, yogurt, and snacks. It was full of food to feed a kid and his family.

Slamming the fridge door, I grab the bottle opener from the drawer and get the cap off for an aggressive sip of beer. Looking at the bottle, I see it's the specialty beer from Matchbox, one of my favorites.

The silence in my place plus the empty fridge are not the reminders I particularly care for right now. Looking over into the living room, I notice the vacant spot on the side table where that rodent lived in a cage, and I have yet to return my antique chess board to its location.

Already I know that heading to bed for the night will be just as grueling. I will only think even more of Sadie. I cancelled the cleaner for the week, because admittedly, I don't want the smell of Sadie off my sheets, and apparently, I turned quite animalistic thanks to her. But a smart man knows that I'm prolonging the inevitable.

Leaning against the counter, I tap the bottle with a finger as I contemplate if I should just give in and go shower with thoughts of Sadie on my mind or if I should try cold turkey on my Sadie detox.

I haven't had this problem before. Normally, I'm the one ending things. I don't involve emotions. It's always been just sex. The moment I thought the woman was catching feelings, I cut the rope. I'm the one calling the shots.

Sadie has turned the tables on me.

I can't even say how I make it to my bedroom, as my mind has only Sadie on replay. Her cute little giggle, her sparkly eyes, and the lines of her body that my fingers love. Then there's the way she just listens, and I can say anything to her without needing to overthink it.

When I peel off my clothes and slide into bed, I stare aimlessly at the ceiling with an audible exhale.

A sour taste hits my mouth at the thought of Sadie in the future with some asshole she'll marry and have beautiful babies with. Rolling to my side, I open the bedside drawer, and the corners of my mouth tug when I pull out the Tiffany's box with the fake engagement ring that looked so perfect on Sadie. Fuck, it looked amazing on her hand as I made her come too.

Placing the box back in the drawer and turning the light off, I make a mental note to return the damn thing.

Rubbing my face, I groan as I fall back into bed.

———

I scrunch up the paper that was lying on my desk, and I throw the wadded-up ball to the other side of the room out of frustration. The whole week, I've struggled to focus. Sadie and I haven't spoken since she told me her decision. She sent me a text saying she would leave my key and credit card with the doorman in an envelope, and when I asked how she was, she responded that it's best if we don't talk for a while.

Maybe it's a cowardly thing to do, but I haven't texted again. What can I say to her?

"Hello, dear brother," my sister chimes as she walks into my office with extra bounce in her step. She smiles as she makes herself comfortable in the chair in front of my desk.

"Oh, today's the day you were coming in," I remind myself. Looking up, I can see my sister looks extra made-up today, nearly an untired human but not quite.

"It is. I get exactly two hours of me time before I meet Steve with the kids. Mason is spending some quality bonding time with Steve while they walk with the twins. Thought I would drop by quickly before I get in some shopping. So, how are things?" She drags out that question.

"Fine. Why wouldn't they be?" I try and focus on my computer screen.

"I just notice you're a little tense." Her tone is slightly annoying, as she's prying.

With vigor, I type a quick get-it-done e-mail to some traders. "Not tense. Just busy."

When I look up, my sister rests her hands on her lap and gives me a stern eye. "So, we're going to play it like that, are we?"

"Again, just busy." The disdain in my voice runs strong.

"You miss having Mason around?"

I can't help but let the corners of my mouth curve up. "You mean my nephew who left Legos all around my place, changed my favorite list on television to some show about superheroes and dinosaurs, and left cookie crumbs in his bed?

Sure." Before my sister can answer, I continue on for some reason, avoiding my sister by clicking my mouse and focusing on the screen. "I mean, at least he used the pool that I forget sometimes I have, and the hamster was kind of cute. Having Mason around also gave me an excuse to leave the office on time, you know, to make it home for reading and dinner."

Zoe clears her throat. "Right. Dinner with Mason… and Sadie."

Just the sound of her name shoots this feeling through me, and it's unexplainable. The feeling I can't identify, it's new. It's near my heart.

I freeze behind my computer. Looking up at my sister, I wait for her next words. The twin gene between us just means I know she's trying to make a point.

"It's okay to say you enjoyed the whole family-waiting-for-you-at-home scenario. I know it goes against your life plan, but well, plans change. And I love that you enjoyed time with Mason. We will always be grateful, but he's only your nephew. You can still have all of that with your own child one day."

I shake my head at her.

Zoe holds her palm up. "Sometimes that involves a significant other that makes you smile, someone you like the idea of spending time with forever."

"I know, Zoe, I'm the one who's been married before, remember?" I lean back in my chair and cross my arms.

"That wasn't a real marriage, Logan. You were young and completely hyped up in the moment. Wasn't true love, anyhow."

I look at her, skeptical and curious. "What's your point?"

A knock on my office door interrupts us, and Jen walks in.

"Hey, Zoe, good to see you." She greets my sister then turns her attention to me. "Sorry to interrupt, I need to quickly check two things with you."

"No problem. What is it?"

"Can I move the Ives & Wells call to seven pm?" she asks, placing her hand to her hip.

"Why would you even ask, of course." I always have evening meetings with Josh and Noah, who are not only friends but my go-to for PR needs. Though, lately, Josh just gushes about his baby and new wife, which was once irritating, but now I think—well, I think I understand the feeling. Then Noah goes on about Cole's sister Lauren who now works for me, and they're also heading towards a forever happy-ever-after.

"Sorry, it was still in the calendar to keep Thursday evenings free. I guess we did that for when Mason was staying with you. I just thought maybe you still wanted that so you could take the nanny out for dinner." She raises a brow then looks at my sister.

"I told you to not call Sadie the nanny," I remind Jen, because only I can call Sadie the nanny, and normally when it involves something dirty. I shake that thought away. "And, well, no. Not an issue, you can change my schedule back to the way it was before the summer." I realize I sound agitated at that thought, because truth be told, leaving the office early to return home to Sadie cooking in my kitchen was a great way to utilize my calendar.

My sister and personal assistant look between one another, and I know this is bad news for me.

"Dinner with Sadie could be nice," my sister mentions.

"Or not, since we want different things and she doesn't even want to speak to me ever again," I admit and realize that I let too much information slip.

My sister hops up from her chair and points a finger at me. "Hah, so you two *are* on a break and have fallen out. I thought so."

"What do you mean on a break?"

"Well, we all know you were happy the past weeks due to a particular reason, and well, this week you're a miserable asshole," Jen explains.

"Again, busy with work. Plus, a break would imply that we're getting back together. That chance is out the window. She never wants to see me again." Frustrated with that thought, I swing around in my chair to look out at the view through the window. I can understand Sadie needs space from me, but she seems actually angry with me.

"Well, if anyone can charm their way back into the good books, it's you. Maybe you should give it a shot. This summer, you've been different, energized, happy, and... I don't know, but it's been good to see... Anyhow, I should go."

"Me too," Jen adds, "I want to get home on time since I have someone at home making me a romantic dinner, waiting for me." I can hear the taunt in her voice.

I ignore their statements. "Fine. Oh, and what was the second thing you wanted?" I ask.

"Oh yeah, I got an invoice from Tilly's, the gift shop we normally order from for... well erm, you know, and they say you sent a fruit basket the other day. I didn't realize, otherwise I would have arranged it for you. Anyhow, I need to pay the invoice but need your approval."

This piques my interest, and I immediately twirl to face the two women. "I didn't order anything. Who did it go to?"

"Sadie."

My stomach sinks, and I have a bad feeling.

"Damn, they probably sent you the invoice instead of

me," Zoe says." "They must've gotten confused that I made the order," my sister explains as she adjusts her purse on her shoulder.

"What do you mean?" I stand up, now urgently needing answers.

"I sent Sadie a fruit basket as a thank-you for her help this summer with Mason." My sister looks at me like I've gone crazy.

My hand finds my forehead. *Oh no.* Tell me she didn't get a fruit basket, my jackass signature move.

"Ouch," Jen says, turning to Zoe with a painful look on her face. "My guess is you didn't mean the card to say *Sadie, Thanks for your help this summer. Take Care, L. Jax*?"

"Well, I did ask them to send that, but to sign it Zoe Jax," she replies.

I rub my face, and I'm furious with the gift shop. They will never see my business again. No wonder Sadie was frosty with me. She thinks I sent her the basket. Whether we have a future or not, there is no way I'm going to let her think that I would send her a damn fruit basket with a simple note.

Not when she's worth so much more than that.

I grab my suit jacket from the back of my chair, needing to find Sadie right this second. "Jen, clear my schedule. I need to sort this out."

"No problem." Jen rushes off, and my sister clears her throat.

I stop in my tracks to look at my sister who is again giving me that look that tells me she has a point to make.

"Are you really going to just say the card was sent in error, or are you actually going to tell her how you feel?"

I sigh then bite my inner cheek, unsure how to answer.

"She wants it all, Zoe," I remind her, and I'm not sure why, but for the first time, I realize that Sadie can have it all, *I* can give that. It's more the question of whether I *want* to give it all.

My sister walks toward me and squeezes my arm. "I think you know that you want it all too. You're a smart man, a successful man, a charmer with a list of women who have received fruit baskets—but for once, you hate the idea of one particular woman receiving a fruit basket. And you know why…" Zoe walks ahead of me and leaves me to sink into my thoughts in the middle of my office.

But I don't need to think long. Sadie doesn't stand a chance.

LOGAN

I knock relentlessly on the door of Sadie's place, hoping that she's there. I've never actually been here, only dropped her off a few times.

The door opens, and my momentary feeling of relief sinks to a feeling of panic when I see a man leaning against the door eating an apple. He looks to be around my age or a few years younger, shirtless too, with running shorts and shoes on, which doesn't help my imagination of who this guy is. His ruffled hair and peak fitness level have me wondering how long he has been shirtless in the place where Sadie lives, where Sadie sleeps.

"Who are you?" The unhappiness is clear in my tone.

The man doesn't flinch and instead bites loudly into his apple as he stands there just staring at me.

My eyes bug out at him while I wait for an answer.

He answers with a full mouth, "The brother who is eating the apple from the fruit basket that my sister's jackass former boss sent her."

Of course. Her big brother is here at the exact moment that I don't need any added complications.

My fingers pinch the bridge of my nose, and I gather a moment to figure out how to play this.

"Look, Wes—"

"Whoa, we are not exactly on a first-name basis yet, *Logan.* We just met, and quite frankly—although my sister hasn't said exactly what happened—her face tells me enough, and I can only imagine what went down. So, *Logan,* you have thirty seconds to explain to me what the hell is going on—and keep in mind that I played varsity football in high school." Wes gives me a devious grin and steps out of the way to allow me inside.

Following him to the living area, I admire the place. It's loft-style, big and open, an ideal bachelor pad.

"Where's Sadie?" I ask in an urgent tone.

"Not here," he states, putting a shirt on.

"Yeah, I gathered. So where is she?" Impatience runs strongly in my tone.

Wes stands there studying me. "She wanted to get some air, which is good since she's been pretty dismal the last few days."

"Fuck." The last thing I want to hear is how upset Sadie is.

"Listen, Logan, my sister is special. Since she mentioned you have a sister too then you know I'm critical of you. Every fiber inside me is telling me to warn you away from her so she can move on."

I hold my hand up and decide to get a little ruthless in this conversation, and I step in his direction. "Look, *Wes*, she isn't going to move on. Not with anybody but me. You're right, she is special. What she and I have is special, and hell, the future with her will be special. We had a misunderstanding, and now I need to know where the fuck she is so I can straighten it out, because I swear if she doesn't go to bed happy tonight then I am not above murdering someone right now."

Wes looks at me in a way that I can hope is impressed, with his brows raising. "It's not a game."

"I know. It's the real deal, so tell me where she is so I can go to her," I nearly grit out.

Wes doesn't answer, instead crossing his arms, and again he investigates me. "Not telling you… Do you love her?"

No hesitation. My crazed car ride over clarified the situation for me. "Yeah, I do."

"She wants the whole marriage and family thing one day. I won't let her settle for anything less. It's all she has gone on about since she was a kid playing with her dolls. We aren't super close, but something tells me adult Sadie hasn't changed."

My eyes don't blink as I hold a standoff with Wes. "None of us will be settling. We will both have exactly what we want, so tell me where the fuck she is?"

Wes's lips form an amused grin. "Someone's touchy. Listen, I'll tell Sadie you stopped by—"

I roll my eyes and sigh. "I'm serious, Wes, I want to make this right and give her everything."

"Yeah, but the big brother in me knows I should talk with her first to see if she actually wants to see your arrogant face again. Then she'll probably say she isn't sure, but you seem like the guy who'll find her anyway. Then she'll give you another chance because that's just her. All the while, I will be watching your every fucking move until the day I'm convinced you're good enough. Then maybe, just maybe, we can sit down where you owe me a beer."

"I'm sure we'll be the best of friends," I say, sarcastic and annoyed. "Haven't you ever felt that way about someone, where you feel like you're about to lose your mind?"

I catch Wes off guard, and he looks off in the distance before returning his gaze to me. "Sure, but I respect their boundaries when they say they need space." The man clearly understands my pain but won't admit it.

"Fine, but if you won't tell me, then I'll just wait for her. Or I could call Ruby." It comes out of my mouth, and it dawns on me that it's a good idea. Pulling my phone out, I quickly type Cole a text and ask for her number; he does business with her father so he must have the intel I need.

"Nope. Don't do that." Wes is adamant and quickly pulls his phone out and must be skimming his contacts for a number to beat me to the punch, then curses when he realizes that he doesn't have the number.

Meanwhile, my phone pings, and his eyes jolt to my phone. "Don't fucking do it," he warns me.

I don't even flinch and hit my screen.

"Hello?" Ruby's voice answers.

"Hi, Ruby, it's Logan. Long time… listen, I need to be quick. Have you spoken to Sadie recently? Hopefully today? I need to find her to surprise her, and yes, I know I may not be your favorite person right now, but trust me, I'll make it right."

"Don't tell him, Ruby!" Wes calls out in hopes Ruby hears.

"Is that Wes? Are you at Sadie's place? Well, this is all a surprise," Ruby answers.

"Please, Ruby," I plead, and all three of us pause.

"I did speak to her, actually…" I'm hoping she'll tell me but can hear her debating.

I breathe out an audible breath. "Please."

"I shouldn't get involved, but she's miserable, and if you don't make it right then I have no problem hunting you down… The library. She went to pick up her staff card for when she starts her job and was supposed to meet me for drinks later."

"Thanks, I owe you," I quickly say then hang up.

Instantly, I walk back toward the front door.

"She isn't coming back here tonight, okay?" I call back to Wes, a little too confident and casual.

Wes growls before he scratches his cheek. "Are you fucking kidding me right now? Did you really just say that to me? You really are an arrogant asshole; you know that, right? I fucking hope my sister found some redeemable feature in you, since she seems to like you." We glance at each other, and I see a wave of reality hit Wes. He knows I'll find Sadie and make it right.

"Don't hurt her."

Stopping at the door, I look back at him. "It's the last thing I ever plan to do."

27

SADIE

Stepping out from the library, I breathe in the summer air. I look around at the various people sitting on the steps and camped out next to the fountain while eating snacks or talking. I glance at my staff card; I decided to collect it today and meet a few new colleagues before I start next week. I wanted the distraction, but it didn't work at all.

My eyes glance to the street as I adjust my bag, and I blink several times, trying to register the scene in front of me —a silver Aston Martin with a very confident-looking Logan leaning against the car, his dress-shirt sleeves rolled to his elbows and his sunglasses on.

I don't understand why he's here or how he knew I was here—or why he has to look like a sweltering piece of hotness—but he's here.

Very slowly and reluctantly, I walk toward him, and he lifts his sunglasses off his head then throws them into the open window of the passenger door.

"Logan, what are you do—"

"Your brother isn't a fan of me, but I got there in the end."

It dawns on me that he must have gone to the apartment when Wes was there.

He propels off the car and steps toward me to close our distance faster. "It's not from me."

I shake my head, confused, as I don't understand what he's talking about.

"The fruit. It wasn't me. My sister sent you the basket, and the shop wrote the card wrong."

My eyes widen from this fact, and I freeze in my spot as I register that piece of information. I don't move as he places a hand on my cheek.

"Y-you didn't send the basket?" I stagger out then gulp as my nerves hit me in full force.

He shakes his head no. "You are so much more than a few bananas and apples."

The corners of my mouth tug at his choice of words. "I'm a little relieved, but it doesn't change—"

His other hand comes to my face to force me to look into his eyes.

"Everything changed the moment I met you, Sadie. The last week has been miserable. Tell me it was just as miserable for you?"

"It was, but—"

"No buts, Sadie. I'm miserable because you aren't waiting for me when I get home. I'm miserable because I don't have toys lying on the floor to trip over or a schedule to adjust because I have a family waiting. It's all I see in my head now, a future with a wife, kids, and fuck it, even a hamster. There is one condition, though." His words come out with so much conviction, and I hear the truth in his tone.

My pulse races, and I feel like I'm about to jump off a cliff, my adrenaline really kicking in. It's what I want to hear.

It's *exactly* what I want to hear, which is why I'm trying to take in the moment and figure out if this is a dream or not.

"What's the condition?" I wonder, still in a semi-daze.

"You. I only want those things if it's with you. It has to be you. I'm in love with you." He leans in, letting our foreheads touch before brushing his lips along my temple.

My heart feels like it's lifting out of my chest. It's pounding so loudly that he must hear it.

The brushing of his lips along my jawline brings me back to the moment. "Tell me it's you. Tell me we go all-in, because I am completely in love with you."

There is no denying it anymore, this isn't a dream.

I don't say anything, instead I step back to study his face. One look and that damn charming grin is telling me this is the real thing. All hesitation floats away, and I move in to capture his mouth. My lips touching his gives him my answer, and he takes over leading us. Logan kisses me almost as if he's punishing me, but I feel the smile as his lips move with our tongues dueling; they clearly missed one another.

"I want it all to be you, I'm in love with you too," I whisper between parting lips and finding a new angle.

We kiss and kiss some more, making up for the days without.

"Hey, you can't park here." A man shouting behind us makes us break our reunion. We both look to the police officer standing over Logan's car. "This is a tow zone, so move it." The policeman hitches his thumb over his shoulder to indicate we need to move. He seems like he's not in a forgiving mood.

"Will do, Officer, just had an emergency to handle," Logan answers, with his fingers waving in the air.

"Public indecency isn't an emergency, now get out of here before I write you a ticket." I can hear the very subtle humor in the officer's voice, although he tries to maintain the grumpy and stern persona.

"We're leaving," I call out.

I grab Logan's hand, and we walk the few steps towards his car, and the officer walks away.

"He might as well write me a ticket for how fast I plan on getting us home," Logan mumbles into my ear before he opens the passenger door, and I can only laugh.

———

LOGAN KEPT true to his word and got us to his place in record time. The whole time he kept our hands interlaced on the middle console, and for the most part, we didn't talk. We had giddy smiles on our faces as we glanced at one another, with my entire body warm and ready.

Logan threw his car keys at the valet of his building when we arrived, and we rushed to the elevator. As soon as the doors closed, our mouths devoured each other with haste. We should definitely talk more, but our bodies have other plans.

Finally, when we manage to get through the front door of his place, it feels impossible to hold it in anymore. Logan lifts me up and plants me on the side table next to the door, quickly peeling my panties down and off, bunching my dress around my waist.

"I need you right now," he speaks against my mouth as I work the buckle of his pants. I'm not going to argue, because I have the same urgency.

We're like two possessed souls overcome with need and desire.

He doesn't even pull his pants and boxers all the way down. I tilt my hips, and he holds the head of his length to my entrance, sliding into me with purpose. Wrapping my arms around him, I pull him close as he moves inside me unapologetically. The side table shaking on every pump, my own grunts fusing with his as he goes deep, all the way until he bottoms out.

Only after we both unravel in our climax does he carry me to his bed without letting us part until he lays me on the bed and collapses next to me.

"I'm never looking at that table the same way again," I admit, still trying to catch my breath from all the excitement.

"I hope you look at it favorably, because I now realize it's perfectly located for those times I can't wait a second longer," he says, lying on his side with a propped elbow.

I smile at him, and I manage to gather all my thoughts.

"What changed your mind?" I wonder aloud.

His fingers comb through my hair while he has a gentle smile on his face. "I didn't change my mind, Sadie, it's a feeling. The real thing. I never wanted a future with someone because I never had this feeling. Until I met you."

I lean up to kiss him quickly on the mouth. "I was already in too deep with you, and that's why I pushed you away," I explain.

He moves to hover over me and trap me in. "Although effective, never do it again. I was losing my damn mind," he warns me before nuzzling into my neck with a little teeth action, nibbling the base of my throat.

"And now?"

"I'm never letting you go. I need you here waiting for me when I come home and when I wake up too. I want you to text me while I'm in a meeting, telling me about your day and what you're buying at the supermarket, what you'll be wearing when you're waiting for me to return home."

"Truly domesticated," I tease as I squeeze our embrace tighter together.

"You've settled me down." He grins before kissing my forehead.

I have to laugh at his thought. "I hope not, because you have the opposite effect on me when we're in bed," I warn him as I roll us, so I'm straddling him and begin to swirl my pelvis on top of his cock.

He has a deep warning laugh before he wraps his arms around my waist and comes to sitting. "We're clearly not leaving this bed for the rest of the day."

I shake my head with a smile.

His fingers brush through my hair, our eyes staring into each other's. Our moment slows down after the last few minutes of passionate and effective make-up sex.

"I love you," he whispers again.

"I love you too."

We lie there, and already I feel it in my body and soul, that this is the first of many times that we will lie like this, completely in agreement of the only direction where we're heading.

"I'm happy you ended up being the nanny and not some old lady."

"Uhm, thanks, I guess."

He chuckles at my response. "I just mean that this was all a good coincidence that you ended up being the nanny, right?"

I brush my fingertips along the tightened muscle of his arms. "Were you not confident that your business card and charm would have persuaded me otherwise?"

"No way, I would have found you again and charmed my way, but this was way more fun."

"Right, because you're always a big charmer," I taunt him, and his eyebrows raise to question me, but then my straight face breaks because it's true. "You wore me down until I couldn't resist."

His finger taps my nose. "You'll never be able to resist me."

The thing about this man is he can be cocky, but deep down, he doesn't take himself too seriously.

"Never is a long time," I mention.

He lowers his mouth to mine. "Exactly. A long time."

EPILOGUE: LOGAN

ONE YEAR LATER

Arriving home, I head to the kitchen, loosening my tie and throwing it on the counter. Grabbing a water from the fridge, I walk to the windows to admire the view of the city, the sun setting to the west creating that perfect pink sky.

It's unusually quiet, which means my new wife must be late getting home from volunteering, extra hours on top of her work at the library where she reads to kids with a dog present. Apparently, it relaxes them.

The warm hands sliding from my spine around to my front confirm that she is in fact home.

"There you are." I swerve around to pull Sadie into my arms. Our fusion of a welcoming kiss and murmur gets us lost in the moment. I love that she's in a loose tank top and a skirt—it's knee-length, but I'll let that go.

"Yeah, here I am." Her voice is light and her face glowing.

"How was your day?" I ask, my hand caressing her cheek.

"Well, it was a big day with what I think is some news,"

she begins and takes my hand, walking me slowly toward the sofa.

"What, Emily told you she slept with your brother?" It flies out of my mouth since Wes now hangs out with me and Cole, so I'm privy to the latest gossip.

Sadie quickly looks at me, surprised, with her eyes blinking a few times. "Wait, what?"

Crap. That was clearly not the news she meant.

"Oh, uh, just joking."

"Right, well, we'll talk about that later." She quickly ignores that sidestep on my part. *Thank God.*

In that moment, I realize that Sadie is absolutely different today.

"Are you okay? You seem a little off. Normally this is when you would rip my shirt off or bite me as I remind you that I need to look respectable for the office," I remind her, pulling her even closer to me.

"Right, so I got the wedding photos back, and they look perfect."

We married in a small ceremony at the place where we met. Sadie planned everything, and I just agreed because I had no preferences or requests. Wait, I take that back—I planned one thing. The white lacy lingerie set that was waiting in a box for her the morning of our wedding with a note requesting her to wear it on our wedding night. She did, and she slayed me that night.

"Ah yes, our perfect wedding. See, we never deceived my clients in the end," I quip, and she playfully pinches me.

"That's why you proposed to me?"

"No, baby, I proposed because it was Valentine's Day and I wanted to be a cliché. You and me in bed after a sweet love-making session. The type of lovemaking that was smooth, sensual, and the image of a perfect montage, complete with a good song. The best part?" I prompt her.

She gives me a knowing look. "I now wear the ring you originally got me when I was just the nanny?"

"Exactly. How many guys can say their engagement ring was on their future missus the first time they fucked? It's kismet." I shrug playfully before Sadie tugs me behind her to the sofa. Her ring flashes a sparkle on our linked fingers.

I've basically only ever seen Sadie with my ring on her finger, from the beginning of our relationship. But seeing our hands entwined with our wedding rings against the backdrop of our mattress just revs my engine and testosterone level. It sends us into so many rounds of sex that I'm beginning to wonder if I should be concerned that my dick might fall off.

"Want to know what else may be kismet?" she asks.

"Surprise me."

Sadie has me sit on the sofa, and she sits on top of me, straddling me and unintentionally teasing my cock, reminding me that I know I need to be energized for the night ahead. I have been trained for this. What I'm not trained for is a white stick being waved in front of my face.

Whoa.

Fuuuck.

The time has come.

"I haven't looked, I'm too scared." The radiant smile on her face only confirms that she isn't scared in *that* way. Well, she might be scared about the chance of twins, but let's just take this one step at a time.

She stares at me because I don't respond. My throat feels a little croaky, and it's possibly because my jaw is open and air fills my mouth.

"Logan, are you okay?" She sounds concerned.

She's asking me if I'm okay? *Christ, man, get it together.*

Step up. Be there for her, it's her body that's going to morph into a hormonal overload of pregnancy that will probably make her tits grow like crazy and her libido skyrocket. No complaints from me on any of those counts.

I clear my throat. "Uhm, yeah. I mean, it's a surprise but not a surprise." Somewhere between sex in the Wisconsin National Park and sex in the honeymoon suite, we decided that we have no need for birth control and flushed those pills down the toilet.

"You look, please," she pleads as she hops to standing between my knees, and in that moment, everything sinks in.

I look at her and warmth fills me. A smile graces my lips, and my hand grabs the stick from her fingers with our eyes not breaking contact.

"Ready?" I ask, and she nods.

My heart races as I flip the stick and look, and then I peer up at her. Pulling her closer to me as I sit on the edge of the cushions, I nuzzle into her stomach.

"Our little boy or girl is in there." I sound emotional.

I hear her breath catch before her beaming smile forms, complete with a few tears quickly emerging from her eyes. She pushes me back to leaning against the sofa and straddles me again.

"We're having a baby." Her voice is feathery and light.

"Yeah, Sadie. Yeah, we are."

Our deep, warm kiss confirms the news, and we sit there for a few minutes, soaking it all in.

"We should order in some dinner, and I think I have a bottle of alcohol-free champagne somewhere in the fridge."

Her mischievous grin comes out, and she tilts her head to the side, her fingers toying with my shirt. "*Or* we could celebrate a different way."

"Something in mind?" I ask her knowingly as I watch her

pull her shirt up and off. Quickly, she unclasps her bra, her beautiful globes already teasing me.

"Very much so." Her hands guide my own to cup her breasts. As if I need guidance—*crazy*.

"You're insatiable, you know that?"

She's already grinding against me when her hair and head fall back, exposing a large playing field for me.

"Yeah, and you did this to me. You convinced me from day one to be very unprofessional because you are the best kind of trouble." She returns to kiss my neck.

I am pretty good at what I do, and for her, I will do anything.

THANK YOU

Readers. Well, you simply rock and I can't tell you how much it means to me that you read my words. I hope you enjoyed the fun little ride of Logan and Sadie. Literally, I woke up one day and it was in my head ready to land on a keyboard.

Kimberly from Revision Division, thanks for beta reading so I could double check I am not going down a (too) crazy path.

Lindsay, for editing my crazy journey. Thanks for continuing to press on with my grammar during unusual times. Always such a breeze to work with too. Those commas still surprise me!

Lindsey, for nailing the cover from the start. Big thank you.

ARC and bookstagram readers, thanks so much all that you do to help promote. Can't release a book without you!

My significant other and offspring, thanks for letting me head off into my corner to write. This is what happens after thirty something years of no coffee then suddenly starting the drink… steamy books. I know you're *totally* excited about this.